Signing Up for Love

Alexis Hawks

Contents

Dedication

This book is dedicated to the man who loves me in all the right ways. ILY Paul.

And to the friend who supports me no matter what shenanigans I get up to, this one's for you, Trenna.

About the Author

Alexis Hawks is a Metis author residing in the Treaty 6 territory on the prairies of Canada—where the long winters gave her plenty of time to fall in love with reading, and eventually, with writing stories of her own.

With a unique voice, she weaves humor into her storytelling while exploring themes deeply connected to her culture and personal journey of reconnection. Alexis lives in Saskatoon with her husband and two children, drawing inspiration from her experiences and surroundings.

When she's not crafting stories, Alexis immerses herself in various cultural activities, enjoys watching her son's parkour lessons, and is usually curled up with a cup of tea, a good book, daydreaming about her next story (and possibly eavesdropping for dialogue ideas—fair warning!).

Trigger Warning

This book contains content that some readers may find distressing or triggering. It discusses sensitive and potentially traumatic themes related to residential schools, Indigenous issues, and acts of violence that Missing and Murdered Indigenous Women and Girls (MMIWG) often experience.

Readers who have experienced trauma related to these topics or are sensitive to such material are advised to proceed with caution. The book includes:

- Mention of residential schools
- Explorations of systemic racism and its impact on the Indigenous
- Kidnapping and violence related to kidnapping
- Some racism expressed towards characters may evoke strong feelings or thoughts.

If you find any part of the content overwhelming or need support, consider reaching out to mental health professionals, counseling services, or support groups within Indigenous communities. Your well-being is important, and seeking help can provide comfort and guidance through challenging material.

Should you want to learn more about colonial impacts on indigenous people, a good starting point is the Truth and Reconciliation website https://nctr.ca/

Should you want to support Indigenous healing, you can support the Indian Residential School Survivors Society https://www.irsss.ca/.

Chapter 1

Nika really didn't want to be here.

But here she was, feeling claustrophobic amongst a crowd of single men and women, all eyeing each other like they were either meat or butchers in a BBQ competition. Was she juicy enough? After all, she had curves for days, probably too many curves, but it had been a long journey to loving herself, and she didn't entertain such thoughts anymore. She must be going crazy to allow those thoughts back in.

Suddenly, she saw Jessie. Her face lit up, and unbeknownst to her, but several people in the crowd noticed, she glowed with a beauty that was both alluring and comforting. She was the Veronica to Jessie's Betty. Jessie was slim, athletic, and wholesome, while she was mysterious, exotic, and perhaps a tad intimidating.

"Hey Jessie!" she raised her hand. "Over here!"

Several faces, men and women, turned to look at her, and she struggled not to feel overwhelmed by the sudden attention.

Jessie rushed up, talking a mile a minute as she usually did.

"You wouldn't believe the traffic! I thought I would be late, which would have worked in my favor since I thought I would puke! Do I look okay? Maybe I should go home and change."

"Don't you dare! You wanted to try this speed-dating thing; it was YOUR idea. If I'm here, you are here, and you look beautiful. I think I'm the one who doesn't fit in here."

"Oh, you! You will be fine once you have a glass of wine and settle in for the ride; you are solid, you know that. It's my turn to buy, isn't it? White or red?"

"I saw some people talking about the wine; it's sketchy at best; go for the rosé."

"Seriously? Sweet? You know me, I like it dark and bitter."

"The red is corked, I think. Just awful from the faces I see and the glasses being tipped or left off."

"Rosé it is. I'll be right back. When does it start?"

"They gave the 15-minute warning just before you arrived."

"Oh my god, and we still need to compare notes!"

She watched Jessie run over to the bartender to give her order while she tugged off her jacket. Nika felt something brush against her as she heard a deep "Sorry" from behind. She turned to look and apologize, but the stranger was gone. Nika hoped she would run into him at the tables; she liked the deepness of his voice. God, why did she let Jessie talk to her about these things?

Jessie and she were BFFs, the best of best friends. They both worked as accountants for a major accountancy firm, Jessie, which specialized in corporate tax returns, while she focused on more forensic accounting. She liked the challenge of finding things and solving puzzles. When they met on her first day of work, both she and Jessie were wearing the same sweater. Instead of taking that as a sign of contention, they bonded immediately over fashion, shoes, being single ladies, and, of course, dreaded dating.

"Rosé it is! I asked the bartender, and he pretty much agreed with you. He said the white was better than the red, but not much better; it had a metallic aftertaste." Jessie shoved a glass in her hand. "So what do you think?"

"Well, lots of interesting men and women here. I suppose it takes all kinds; there are millennials, older people; I think I spotted a goth or two, some fitness freaks, some tattooed rebels, perhaps a circus performer, and some librarians and cat ladies."

Jessie laughed. "Well, better them than us! Anything catching your eye?" "No," Nika replied "But oddly enough, something caught my ears. Someone pushed past me and apologized, and I liked what I felt—a pleasant, deep voice, it had rumble." "Ohhhh" Jessie sighed "It's always good when it has rumble." They laughed together, relaxing.

"Are we looking for men or ladies tonight?" Jessie was one of the few people who knew I was bisexual.

"When I filled out my card, I did mention my orientation, so we will see what I get. They've assigned us all to a calendar of tables based on our applications and when we will be at those tables. So maybe Table 17 at 9:45 will be my lucky star."

Just as we both laughed, a woman with a clipboard approached Jessie. "Jessie Casperden?" "Yes, Ma'am!" "Here's your itinerary. Please be at those tables at those times. We will ring a bell and yell switch so you will know to change tables." Shifting her attention to me, "You know to keep an eye on Troy for those shift changes?" "Yes, Ma'am," I responded.

She winked and, as she turned away chirped gaily, "Have a great time, ladies."

"They've really thought of everything, haven't they?" Jessie leaned in and said to me.

"Yes, and now I can choose who I want to out myself to and who I don't."

"To the golden unicorn!" Jessie laughed.

Chapter 2

Jessie honestly didn't see anything as a barrier. She was aware of her privilege; it wasn't like she was ignorant. She just honestly saw everything that made me unique as something grand, wonderful, and beautiful. It was part of what really gave me the power to see myself that way. I knew deep down that I was a bit of a mismatch, but thanks to Jessie, I was confident that it wouldn't matter.

Sometimes, though, I struggled with myself, and doing these little exercises was no exception. After all, who wants to date a Metis, bisexual, deaf, Rubenesque girl? I was curvy, I was a social justice warrior in my spare time, and I was angry and at peace all at the same time. I was hurt and waiting for more hurt, but I was hopeful. Sometimes life just got fucking messy.

"Earth to Nika! They've run the first bell! Good luck!"

She watched Jessie run off to potentially find her soulmate at Table 7 while she made her way to Table 12, where a frizzy-haired, bespectacled man nervously chewed his fingernails. She plastered on her best smile while she frantically tried to figure out how not to shake his hands.

"Hi! I'm Nika, and you are? As she slowly placed her drink and notepad down on the table. He stood up and held out his hand. "I'm David," he said in a squeaky voice. "Pleased to make your acquaintance," he stared down at the card and said slowly, "Nika?"

"Yes."

"Is that Russian?"

"Oh no, it is very firmly Metis, and I'm not going to shake your hand until you've hand-sanitized it or washed it. You were chewing your nails as I was walking to the table."

He flushed a slow, deep red and frowned. "Oh, right, I suppose not." He withdrew his hand.

"That's Indian, isn't it?" He said that with that hint of disapproval, you always hear in the voice of someone who found something they didn't want in their burger. Like pickles, my heritage was going to be like pickles for him.

"I distinctly asked for no Metis on my burger." She imagined him shouting at someone.

"I prefer Indigenous or Metis, myself," she smiled, knowing that this wasn't going very well. "Indians are East Asians. The actual intended location Columbus was shooting for, but he missed. Our loss and their gain, I suppose." In for a penny, in for a pound, she figured.

He flushed a deep red again and frowned even further. "Are you one of those people who feel we live on stolen land and all that stuff?"

"You do. There's no feeling about it. You just simply do." She retorted calmly.

"I'll have you know my family has been here for 4 generations."

"Don't care." I cut him off. "Look, let's just agree that this one was a bust, mark our cards down, and make some small talk like we're standing in line at the grocery store. I'll drink my wine, you drink your beer. And we'll make the best of the next 5 minutes."

"God damn shame you're a bitch, you were beautiful."

"Oh, so that's how that is?"

She noticed one of the moderators walking by the table, and their eyebrows shot up to hear his comment. The moderator motioned their head in a "need help?" and she shook her head back. She could handle another five minutes of the guy. She leisurely filled out her card, rating the experience, noting he was trying to see what she was writing, so she put a simple "Not a match, better luck next time" on it. She figured that the moderator would come and find her at some point, and she could share her true reflections on his lack of character at that point.

"I suppose you are one of those 'woke' people." he snidely broke the silence.

"That's our responsibility, is it not? To learn, to explore, to ensure that we are inclusive, and to create a community that has all types and kinds. I'm actually really surprised we were matched, seeing how completely different we are in personality."

He flushed a deep, dark red again. "Well, I'm not having a lot of luck at these, so I may have made some comments that I don't necessarily believe in to try and expand my luck.

"You realize that's not how it works, right? You realize that what you've done is guaranteed your matches will not be a good fit for you."

"But none of them were already a good fit for me."

"Then maybe you should look inside yourself to see why you aren't a good fit for them."

"I'm not the problem here. I know that I'm well off, I'm decent looking, I own my house, I have two cars, my divorce was painless, and she's not in my life because we didn't have kids. I know I'm not the problem."

"None of that list speaks to your personality and character. That's all the stuff. If YOU are the problem, then it's YOU, not what you bring to the table."

The bell rang, and Nika got up with relief. "It was nice to meet you. I'm sorry we weren't a match."

"No, you aren't."

"No, I'm not, but I'm trying to salvage your dignity with politeness. Never mind."

She headed off to Table 23, her next endeavor. Hopefully, this one will go better.

Chapter 3

Several tables and conversations later, she was feeling overwhelmed, stressed, and done with the night. She had met some lovely people and had a laugh with Jessie when they discovered they had been paired together at one point. Jessie mischievously admitted she had also put bisexual on her application just to see what was out there. She was pretty sure she had made a new knitting friend, but struck out on the ladies otherwise. Nika couldn't help but laugh at her friend, and after that short, rejuvenating break, they both took a deep breath and dived back into the dating pool.

That was it; her last table and nothing really stood out for her in terms of conversations or people. She would likely go to that hockey game the one gentleman had invited her to, at least to get out and give someone a chance. But that elusive spark she and so many others were looking for wasn't there.

She sat down at the table. It was still empty, so her next match might have been to get a drink before the timer chimed. She put down her papers and pen and took the time to really think about what she wanted to know from someone else who could possibly be dating material. Did she care about their job? Their home? What hobbies did she want to hear about or not hear about? Okay, maybe not Taxidermy.

Her fourth conversation was about an avid hunter and taxidermist, and she still shuddered when thinking about that conversation. Once he started talking about the process of preserving, she desperately listened while trying to figure out a way to get out of the conversation politely. Finally, she had to admit she had no guts and no glory, and could he please stop before she threw up in his lap? That certainly got his attention, and he laughed, but she was still cringing internally.

A scent of pine wafted behind her, which reminded her painstakingly of back home up north, where the frost was cold, the dark seemed on the edge of everything, and the community rang bright. Her grandparents' cow farm, with the seeming forest of trees that surrounded it, was where she would explore for mushrooms and chokecherries. Her Kokum would talk about the way of the witches, and they would watch the northern lights dance upon the snow in the winter. She sighed, homesick, as someone came from around her and sat in the seat opposite.

Shaken out of her reverie, she stared at him, confused for a second, and then he stared back. He was handsome looking, if in a bit of an unconventional way. His nose had that slight bent as if he'd been in one too many fights; his hands looked big and rough, and the beer glass he held in it seemed small and delicate in his grasp. He had warm chocolate brown eyes and a day-old beard. He cleared his throat, and she started. It was him! The deep-voiced "Sorry" guy. Maybe the evening wasn't a loss after all.

"Oh, uhmmm, hi!" she said brightly. "Sorry, I was stuck in a memory thanks to your cologne. My name is Nika. What's yours?"

"Jason. Nice to meet you. That's a beautiful name. Different." He smiled a kindly, if crooked smile.

"Yes, it is, isn't it?" She smiled softly and couldn't prevent the yawn that escaped.

"Tired? This has been an adventure." He emphasized adventure as though he weren't quite sure whether it was exciting or terrifying.

She laughed. "Oh, it was an adventure, all right. I managed to offend some people and hurt some feelings, and I generally remember why I don't like dating all in the span of mere hours. How about you?"

"I haven't dated in so long. I didn't think I knew how, but then I remembered why I hadn't dated in so long. No one else knows how, either! It was so awkward. At one table, the lady spent the whole time blushing and laughing. I still don't know her name!"

She laughed harder. "Maybe she was hypnotized by your muscles or beautiful brown eyes!"

"Oh, you think I have good muscles and my eyes are pretty?"

She blushed. "Ooops, outed."

"Hey, I'll take it! I couldn't help but notice that you were at another table with a lady earlier. You two sure seemed to be hitting it off and laughing. It couldn't have been all bad!"

"Watching me? Were you?" she laughed as it was his turn to blush.

"Well, yes, but no, you are a striking woman, and your laugh is infectious. Once you start laughing, I can't help but watch you."

"Thank you for the compliment, Jason. I am flattered. But while I am bisexual and open to dating ladies," she watched him intensely to gauge his reaction, "I was actually, funnily enough, paired with my BFF, who convinced me to come to this whole event. We were laughing because while it was a great match, it would never be that kind of match for us. The most we will ever be romantic is as work wives."

"Oh, you two work together? That's cool. So, did you come here looking for men? Or women? Or? "

"I'm here to meet people." She stated firmly. "I think I found a few that will make good friends, but no spark, not yet."

"Well, I'll have to try harder then." He stared straight at her with a serious face.

She blushed and cleared her throat. "Well, anyway, what are you looking for?"

"Me?" He sat back and relaxed. "A connection. I lost my dating mojo, and I just needed to test the waters and get back into it. I'm only into the ladies. I hope you don't mind."

"Me? No, I don't have a horse in that race." He roared with laughter. "I haven't heard that phrase from anyone other than my dad! That's it. I'm sold, and I have to take you on at least one date."

She blushed again and laughed. "Well, I guess we'd better give each other good reviews and maybe exchange contact information to arrange that future date."

"Done and done! Gimme your phone, and I'll program my number into it. Here's my phone."

She tried to think of some witty name to give herself on his phone. Something funny and true to their date, finally, she handed him his phone back.

"Hey, Jason?"

"Yeah?"

"I really enjoyed this little match. Thank you for ending this night on a positive note. I hope to see you around." She grabbed her coat and went off in search of Jessie to crow about her good luck.

Chapter 4

Jessie and she were standing around the coffee maker the next morning at work.

"Tell me again," Jessie said. "You think you met someone worth dating at this?"

She rolled her eyes. "Okay, okay, you were right. Getting out of our routine and trying something new can sometimes be a good thing. I am glad you suggested it. There. Happy?"

"Oh no, I want a dozen donuts delivered to my desk with a huge thank you bouquet. With all the moaning and griping you did up to the event, I'm going to gloat about this for a while." She grinned.

"Oh, come ON, I don't even have a date yet! He hasn't texted, and he may never text. You aren't so successful yet, Missy!"

Suddenly, she felt her phone vibrating in her pocket. She valiantly tried to ignore it, but Jessie must have heard it. "Was that a text? Perhaps from a young, handsome stud you met at a speed dating event last night?"

"What's this about, a speed dating event last night?" Terrell walked into the lunchroom with a curious look in his eye. "Did you try speed dating? God, sometimes I'm just so glad Annie married me, so I don't have to worry about this stuff."

"We did!" Jessie crowed, "And she may have met a handsome man to date! But she's holding her cards to her chest and won't tell me much about it."

"You both went? Wow, how did you two manage to separate long enough to talk to other people?"

"Oh, you! We know how to meet other people! We're only working wives here, and that's because everyone else was already taken." Jessie laughed

Terrell snorted. "I don't have a work wife."

"Yes, you do! It's Nancy! She brings you muffins and coffee cakes all the time."

"That's my work, wife?" He shrugs. "I'll take it. But maybe that's why Annie keeps telling me not to piss off Nancy. She sure likes her banana bread."

Jessie rolls her eyes. "Sometimes you are the most clueless person on the planet. Yes, that's your work, wife."

While they bickered, she checked her phone. "A dark horse? How fitting. Jason here. I was wondering if you wanted to meet for coffee or dinner this Friday. Would you be up for that?"

"Well, I had to think of something witty for you to remember me by. Nika Dark Horse seemed fitting, and yes, I would love to. When and where were you thinking?"

"Do you want to go to the local art gallery? That will give us some conversation starters, and I know they have a coffeehouse attached. We can grab some brew and wander around. Or wander around and grab a brew. I'm not sure if drinks are allowed in the gallery, but they have a coffeehouse in the gallery. You can clearly tell I am out of my element."

"LOL. Sure! That sounds fun. Let's go and see what it's all about. I'm sure it will be a great time."

She looked up from her phone with a little smile on her face and saw Jessie and Terrell staring intensely at her.

"Uhhhhhm," she smiled weakly, "so I have a date?"

Jessie lunged forward and grabbed her by the shoulders.

"Deets! NOW!"

We're just meeting for a coffee at the art gallery. We will look at some exhibits and get to know each other. No biggie."

"Ooohhhhhh," Jessie and Terrell said simultaneously. "The art gallery.... for the exhibits."

"Oh, come on, you two. Quit being over dramatic. Anyway, I have to get back to my desk. That report I'm working on has to be submitted by 4 pm, and it's already 3:15."

She walked away, gripping her phone tightly with a grin on her face. The word GOALLLLLLL reverberated in her head.

Chapter 5

She didn't think Friday would ever get here. But it did. She decided to go chic, wearing a rich plum turtleneck with a tan leather pencil skirt paired with warm suede booties. She topped it off with a beautiful Metis printed scarf and her beaded earrings. She hoped she wasn't the first one to the gallery. Waiting in brightly lit places for your date to show up was excruciating.

As she walked up the steps to the glass building, a warm, beckoning light shone from the windows, she could see Jason just inside the door sitting on a bench with his head cocked to one side as he stared at something on the wall. Jaunting up the steps, she texted him, "Just arrived. I'll be right in."

She watched as he fumbled for his phone, and a smile spread across his face as he looked up at the door, watching for her. That was gratifying to see; he really looked forward to seeing her.

She slipped in and said a breathy "Hello" as he walked up to her.

"Are you cold?" he asked.

"A little, that wind is cutting, isn't it?"

"Well, do you want to walk around and get warm that way? Or grab a glass of something and just talk?"

"What I want is to see what you were looking at while I was coming up the steps. You seemed unsure."

He laughed. "Oh, that! It's right here," He said, leading the way. "I can't figure it out, but I think it's made out of ...hair?" He gave a little shake of his head.

She stared at it, and it seemed as if it was something that felt like a huge hairball. She stared at the accompanying card.

"Well, it does say hair fiber and mixed media. So yes? "

"I don't always get it, but I think that's the point sometimes, isn't it?" Jason laughed.

"I took some art classes at university, and I seem to recall that the important part of art is to evoke a reaction, a feeling, a thought, or just a reaction. So clearly, you reacted. It's done its job. It's not always about understanding the why or what."

Jason nodded. "That makes sense. Art classes, huh? Budding artist?" He motioned at her earrings.

"Actually, my aunt made me these. I didn't. I don't really have an artistic bone in my body; I'm more of an art historian type. I know the details and history. I had to fill those electives somehow!" She laughs.

Jason leads her over to the bar and orders them both a glass of red. "I'm sorry. I should have asked what you wanted."

"I'm okay with red, thanks."

"Good. Anyways, those earrings are beautiful."

"Thank you again. I love them. They are dear to me."

"So, are you close with your family?"

"Absolutely, I grew up really close with all my cousins, aunts, and uncles. I saw my grandparents every weekend. You?"

"Well, not like that, but I'm very close with my mom, dad, and my brother. In fact, I told them that I met this little firecracker at a speed dating event, and my brother is already campaigning for me to join the married couples brigade. He said he can't handle being the only married one, with the bachelor brother making single life look like so much less of a headache." Jason laughed.

Nika blushed at his "little firecracker" comment.

"As flattered as I am, I am hardly little." She flushed.

"You are perfect to me, and compared to me, you seem little." He stopped and stared into her eyes, showing his desire for her in a look.

She blushed harder. "Uhmm, I don't know what to say about that."

"You don't have to say anything at all."

He cleared his throat, turned his darkened eyes toward the next painting, and said, "So, what do you think of this piece?"

She laughed softly, thankful for the reprieve as they slipped into a comfortable camaraderie for the rest of the night, sharing stories, laughter, and the occasional odd look at an installment that didn't make sense.

At the end of the evening, she thanked him for a lovely evening and went home, glowing and happy. Hoping he felt the same.

As she was preparing for bed, she felt the vibration of her phone. Pulling it out of her leggings pocket, she saw a text from him. "Sweet dreams, little firecracker."

She smiled and did indeed have sweet dreams.

Next Monday, around the coffee maker at work, she was regaling Jessie and Terrell with her date with Jason. Jessie was clearly pleased with what she felt was a home run.

"What a great date! Will you see him again?" Terrell asked.

"If he wants to, absolutely."

"Oh, he would be crazy not to." Jessie quipped.

"Speaking of crazy, I had a message from the speed-dating people that one of my matches wanted to get in touch with me. Was that the David guy my first match? The disaster that was racist and a touch homophobic?"

"OH MY GOD," squealed Jessie, "What was the message? Did you get it?"

"Well, I wasn't going to agree to them releasing my contact information, so I told them that I wasn't comfortable doing so, and if he really needed to send me a message, he could do so through them. I then told them about my conversation with him and how uncomfortable it was. They said one of the moderators had overheard bits and pieces and had reported it already."

"So, did he send the message?"

"Oh yeah, they forwarded it to me last night with their apologies."

Jessie and Terrell gasped. "THEY apologized? What did he say?"

"Are you ready for it?"

They nodded.

"Hi, Nokia, I am David, and we met last week at the speed dating event. I have decided that I am willing to consider dating you as long as you lose 15-20 pounds. Only then would you be pretty enough for me to date in a public venue; however, if you wanted to meet privately to get to know each other better, I would be open to that even before you lost the weight. I will overlook the fact that you are Indian as long as you understand that no one is ever to know. You can pass well enough that people wouldn't even realize, as long as you don't tell them. I would also be willing to overlook your bisexuality as long as you bring girls home for both of us and don't go off cavorting without me. I am attaching the contact information of a personal trainer that I feel would benefit you. I look forward to hearing from you in one month if you want a public relationship or even sooner if you want a private one."

Terrell sat back. "Wow, that's bad."

She sighed and flushed. "Like I can't figure out if I'm laughing at this or furious at this. I personally don't understand it. So, a guy is allowed to have a little extra meat on his bones, and we're supposed to idolize the Man Bod. Give him his credit as a person who will keep us warm in the middle of the night. And we put on an extra 15-20 pounds, and we're the worst sort of people that aren't allowed to be pretty or dateable, even?" Nika grimaced at the whole thought.

Jessie groaned. "Block him! Do not respond. God, men are such assholes."

Terrell shook his head. "Men are such assholes." with an aggrieved sigh. "I can't be the only one repping the green flag masculinity."

"Men are such assholes." Nika vehemently agreed while she giggled quietly.

"Well, I've got to get back to work. I certainly hope that the speed dating organization removes him from its client list. That is horrifying. No one should treat another person like this. You are perfect and beautiful the way you are, and I'm proud of your cultural pride." Jessie stood up and hugged Nika fiercely.

Terrell's face had a sudden look of surprise.

"You are.... bisexual?"

"SHHHHHHHH!" Jessie groaned, "That doesn't need to be common knowledge here at work. That's Nika's to decide who and where."

"I did not know! I'm just learning this myself! Color me a little surprised!"

Jessie started dragging Terrell back to their offices when he suddenly straightened and looked back at Nika with a confused expression.

"Wait! Did he call you a cell phone?"

Nika laughed. "Yes, Terrell, he totally did!"

Chapter 6

Jessie stopped by Nika's office a few days later at the end of the day.

"Hey, wifey! Terrell and some of the guys were thinking of hitting up the bar on Friday for drinks. Wanna come? I won't go unless you go, and I'm feeling it. I think I want to go. So... Pretty please?"

"I'm hoping that Jason will ask me out again, but if it's right after work, I can probably do one drink."

"Hey, if he wants to see you, tell him to come by! It'll be fun. I guarantee it!"

"Wait, I smell a trap! You just want to meet and grill him!"

"YES! Do you remember that message you read to us Monday afternoon? Clearly, we need to run interference. The men are running amok."

"Ohmigod. You're going to ambush him."

"Only if he shows up. He can always say no."

"He has to ask me out first, and I have to tell him where I am, but yes, I will go out for drinks after work on Friday."

Friday rolled around faster than expected. By the end of a long day staring at the same four pages of financial transactions, it felt like Nika really needed to get out and laugh with her coworkers. Jessie had chosen a pub downtown, not far from the office. There was one issue with the pub: it had Friday Karaoke, and she just knew Jessie would try to get her up on stage. It seemed a personal challenge for her that she hadn't managed to drag Nika up since that one time in college.

Nika did not sing. She knew it didn't make sense to Jessie, but with her inability to hear very well on the best of days and not at all on the worst of days, she just refused to open herself up to the potential ridicule of karaoke. She knew the ribbing was all in good fun, but for her, it hit a sensitive spot.

She got to the pub and saw the crew sitting at the back tables. They had pushed three of them together. Some of them were talking animatedly about whatever crossed their minds, a few were watching the games on the TVs, and some were just quietly sharing the stresses of the week. She squeezed in between Jessie and Nancy, giving a quick grin to Terrell, who sat across from her with a big plastic-wrapped container on the table beside him.

"What's that?"

"Nancy's banana bread. Annie's suddenly not going to be too upset that I'm having drinks after work."

Nancy laughed. "I know how this works! I had bananas that needed to be used anyway. Tell Annie I said hi and give her a hug for me."

Terrell grinned. "You really are my work wife."

Nancy laughed out loud. "WHAT?"

Jessie laughed and leaned in close. "Nika and I were talking about our dating escapades, and Terrell gave us a hard time about being married to each other. We said you were his work wife, and he was amazed. But now he realizes the truth."

Nancy laughed and shook her head. "I think I need a work wife."

Terrell turned bright red. "Is that me? Am I Nancy's work wife, too? Is she going to divorce me?"

Everyone burst into laughter.

"Buy me flowers, and I'll see how I feel in the morning." Nancy quickly retorted.

Terrell looked panicked. "I don't even do that for Annie. She'll have my head if she finds out I bought you flowers."

Nancy threw her napkin at him in disgust. "Buy your wife flowers! What's wrong with you!"

Suddenly, Nika felt her phone vibrate, and she pulled it out. It was Jason.

"Hey, what's up? Doing anything fun?"

"Hey! Just having drinks with my coworkers."

Jessie looked over her shoulder. "INVITE HIM," she mouthed.

"Sorry, I wasn't around this week. Work kind of exploded, and my brother needed some help after hours. I just don't want you to think I forgot you.

"No worries! I was pretty busy myself."

"Want to meet later this evening after your drinks?"

"You could come to the pub if you feel comfortable. It's a bunch of coworkers, so it's nothing too stressful. Just beer and a couple of sports events on TV. Maybe some karaoke, but only if you allow yourself to get bullied. They smell blood in the water like a shark."

"I could swing by and then maybe take you out for dinner?"

"I'd like that!"

"It's a date! Give me the address, and I'll be there in 20ish minutes."

Jessie hit her shoulder. She looked up to her as she shouted, "YAS GIRL! GET SOME!"

"You hit me?"

"He's coming. This is awesome! I have so many questions."

"You hit me?"

"Terrell, we need to plan how to approach this."

"Jessie! You HIT ME!"

"I'm sorry. I was excited?"

"Okay, you only get 5 questions since you hit me."

"No! I have like 15 already!"

Terrell leans in close. "Do I get five questions?"

Nika, feeling that Terrell couldn't be as bad as Jessie, shrugs. "Sure, why not?"

Terrell grins widely. "Jessie, HAPPY BIRTHDAY! I gift my questions to you."

Jessie crows as a voice pops up in the back of the table. "It's Jessie's birthday? Bartender! Get the lady another drink!" As three other people burst into singing, "Happy Birthday!"

"Shut up! It's not my birthday! Terrell just pregamed it a tad. I'll expect drinks and songs in about 2 months."

People laughed and shrugged as a grinning waitress brought her another drink.

"Oh, lord," Jessie sighed. "I'm going to get drunk tonight." She perks up. "AND I get 10 questions."

"I didn't agree to this!" But Nika couldn't hold back her laughter. Perhaps if Jessie finished another glass of wine, all she could think to ask would be what his favorite cheese was. Jessie sure did love cheese.

Nika settled back and let the various scenarios of how badly or well this could go flow through her mind. This was either a very good idea, like a hazing of sorts, or a sorting hat, you could say. Or this was going to be very, very bad, and she would never see him again.

Suddenly, she felt a hand on her shoulder. "Nika?" She looked up. "Oh, hi, Jason! You made it!"

Terrell perked up. "Jason? Are you Jason? We have heard SO MUCH about you!"

"You have?" said Nika, as Jason simultaneously said, "I hope it was all good."

Jessie stood up and looked at him a little owlishly. Oh, great, the wine was kicking in. "Hi!" she said, holding out her hand. "I'm Jessie, Nika's wife."

"Your...wife?" Jason looks at Nika questioningly. Nika and Terrell exploded in laughter.

"My work wife. This is my best friend who talked me into the whole speed dating thing."

"Oh, I remember you! You were the one laughing with her at that table in the middle of the event."

"YES! THAT WAS ME!" Jessie shouted delightedly. "Now, I have 10 questions for you and have had two glasses of wine. This is going to be fun."

"Oh, is it?" said Jason. "Well, I'm game." As he squeezed in between the two of them.

Jessie sat down, patting his arm. "I think I like you already."

Hours and lots of laughter later, Nika and Jason decided to leave to have supper. As she was putting on her coat, Jason leaned in and said, "I like your work, friends, even your wife." Nika howled with laughter. "Well, I'm glad. I think they liked you. That one joke you told seemed to seal the deal."

"I'm a funny guy."

"That you are."

As they walked out to his truck, he held out his arm for her to hold, and they shared a companionable silence.

Jason cleared his throat and said, "I really like you too. I just wanted to make that clear in case you were wondering."

"You know what, Jason, I like you too."

They continued to make small talk on the way to the restaurant. Once seated and warm with drinks ordered, Jason took a moment to just stare at her.

"What?" Nika asked.

"Just admiring the view. It was a little dark in the pub, and I like looking at you." Nika blushed. "Thank you kindly, Sir!" she laughed with an awkward pause; "I can't take a compliment. I'm sorry, I'll work on that."

"I would like it if you would, because I intend to compliment you a lot." Jason grinned.

She blushed again.

"So I have a question," he said.

"Fire away!"

"You are wearing those beaded earrings again, and they are very beautiful. I can't help but notice them, but I swear they are different colors this time?"

"Yes, I own several pairs. In all ranges of colors." Nika tensed up a bit; she could feel where this was heading, and while she wasn't sure how the conversation would go, she hoped it would go positively. She really liked him.

"Your aunt again? Is this her business? Or just a hobby?"

"It's her business, but I strongly believe in supporting local and cultural businesses."

"Your shirt the other day at the gallery, it said #indigenous. Is that also a part of her business?"

"No. Jason, I can tell what you are trying to get here, and I'm just going to put it out there because I sense you are struggling with asking directly and are unsure how to dance around it." She took a deep breath.

"My family is Metis, I am Metis. I am proud of our Indigenous roots, and I will proudly wear the items that speak of my upbringing. This is who I am."

"I didn't want to offend, but you don't look Metis."

"Jason." She took a deep breath. "What do Metis look like to you? Or maybe I should ask what you know about the Metis."

"Well, you are First Nations or Aboriginal. Are those the correct terms?"

"The Metis are a marriage of Indigenous and White settlers. Usually, French Catholic settlers who came to Canada were completely unprepared for the wild of the land. They intermarried to flourish. I am from the Red River Settlers of Manitoba, in the Winnipeg area. I am Metis on both my mother's and my father's side. We would not consider ourselves to be First Nations. We are Metis. Just like the Inuit, they are not considered First Nations. They are Inuit. Anyways, being of mixed blood, we have just as much of a chance in the genetic lottery of looking white as we do looking Indigenous. I clearly present as white. My sister looks much more Indigenous than I do. She's gorgeous."

"Okay." He nodded, thinking.

"Are you okay with this? If you aren't, that's fine; we walk away, and we don't see each other again. I am who I am."

"NO! No. I'm okay with this. I just think I have a lot of learning to do, and I'm trying to figure out where to start." He looks up hesitantly. "Look, I really like you, but I've never dated anyone who wasn't Caucasian. I've never dated someone that has an identity that I don't understand, and it makes me wonder how to not screw it up."

She laughed softly. "Not screw it up," she repeated softly. "Well, okay, I would call this, not screwing it up. It's okay to ask questions. It's okay to be careful not to offend, and I can help you figure this all out. BUT It is not an Indigenous person's responsibility to teach you about your ignorance. I will teach you because you want to learn, and you are dating me, but with any other Indigenous person, you don't expect them to teach you. It's on you to go out and learn. This isn't a sit-and-wait for them to come to you; it's you who goes out and learns things because it's the right thing to do. If you ever have a question, you can ask me. I'll let you know."

"Is your culture the reason you are so close to your family?"

"Yes. That being said, I grew up with some German/Ukrainian families that are super close at the aunties/cousins level, so you could say it's a symptom of the prairie lifestyle. But yes, many of the Metis families in my community are all super close with the aunties/uncles and cousins."

"I'm close with my mom, dad, and brother, but not that close with anyone else."

"You had mentioned that the other night."

They settled into a thoughtful silence when the server brought their meal. They took the time to start eating and just think about what had just happened.

"Do you speak another language?"

"Yes and No. I speak three languages, but only English well. I speak Michif but not very well. I'm learning; my mother and aunts all speak it really well, and I'm doing my best, but it wasn't spoken in the home for me like it was for my mom and her sisters."

"And your third language?"

"Boy, you are going to go full speed ahead, aren't you?"

"Sorry! I can quit!"

"No! It's all stuff we should probably be talking about on the 3rd date, anyway. This is the third date? Right?"

Jason laughed. "Well, yes, I'd like to add ...and counting to that. "

"Okay, third date and counting," she smiled.

She took another deep breath.

"I also know sign language."

"Oh, is someone in your family deaf?" Jason interrupted.

"Yes. Me."

"What? No, you aren't."

"Yes. I am."

"No way, I'm talking to you right now! You aren't."

"Well, let's do this again. Jason, what does deaf look like to you?"

"Don't deaf people not talk?"

"You mean mute people?"

"No! Every deaf person I've met either doesn't talk or talks funny."

"But funny how? Do you mean funny like a clown? Do I amuse you?"

Jason burst out in laughter. "I don't know if I should be turned on or disturbed right now."

Nika giggled. "Okay, I'm legally deaf. However, I still have functionality. I am completely deaf in my left ear, and I have about 10 percent left in my right ear. My mother and aunties, there's that family closeness again, worked EXTREMELY hard to make sure that I enunciated clearly and talked well. I lip-read and use body language to offset that. I have no issues with asking you to repeat yourself a few times to get it straight, and I think you've noticed that. I also think you've unconsciously noticed that I favor an ear because you make a point of leaning into my good ear to talk to me in loud situations. Even if you haven't realized, on a level, you've known."

"Why was talking clearly so important to them?"

"If I didn't function this well in spite of my disability, do you think I would have the job that I have? The education? The doctors advocated that my mom send me away to an institution for the deaf. Do you have any idea how traumatizing that was for her to hear? Indigenous kids who were taken away and put into residential schools did not fare well. They were abused, they were mistreated, and alienated from their family and their culture. Their clothes were taken away from them, and their identities were erased in favor of turning them into little bland children, even going so far as to change their names to things like Ruth, Franks, Margaret, and Vincent. Whether or not I was taken to a residential school or an institution for the deaf, it still spoke volumes of terror for my family. It was not an option."

"Residential schools were hundreds of years ago!"

"The last residential school was the Gordon's Indian Residential School in Punnichy, Saskatchewan, Jason. It closed its doors in 1996." She looked down at her napkin, feeling hot and mad while trying to stay calm.

"What? 1996? No way."

She shrugged, "I've taught you. Now it's up to you to do your learning. Look it up. Google exists on your phone; I'm going to finish my steak".

She started eating slowly, feeling the slow churn of anxiety, wondering if this was the right path to happiness. It didn't feel very happy now.

She could feel Jason fiddling with his phone. She didn't want to look up. She didn't want to see disbelief in his eyes.

"Holy shit."

He sat back in his chair with a creak.

She nodded thoughtfully while she chewed her steak.

"Are you mad at me?"

"No." She said, "I'm mad at the world that made these conversations necessary. I'm sad that not everything I teach you will be good, fun, or happy. I'm hurt that people hurt my family and my people. I'm many things, but I am not mad at you."

"I'm sorry. I didn't understand," he said quietly.

"Yeah, me too."

Chapter 7

Nika spent the weekend feeling really unsettled about their conversation on Friday night. She knew it was a conversation that needed to be had, and while they left each other that night, laughing and smiling, she couldn't shake the feeling that maybe being so serious so quickly had spoiled things, and perhaps he wouldn't text her again for another date. As much as she liked to pretend that she was strong enough to put her culture, her family, and her identity first, she really liked him, and for tough conversations like these to maybe change how he felt about her, well, that hurt. A lot.

Suddenly, she felt a ding on her phone. She grabbed it out of her pocket quickly. Her shoulders sank when she realized it was Jessie.

"Hey, girl! How was last night?"

"Oh, you know how it is. I came out as Metis and deaf in the span of 20 minutes, so you know. Fabulous?" She added that little shrug emoji to her text.

"You didn't! Oh no, did he take it well? Are you okay?"

"Why do we both assume that's a bad conversation to have? It's not just you. I'm presenting it as a bad news bear thing, too. Why are these conversations not all happiness and light? It wasn't, BTW."

"Do you need me to come over?"

"Nah, I'm relaxing, having a PJ day, trying to figure out how okay I will be if he never texts me back. While the conversation seemed to go okay, it also seemed to be a lot heavier and heated than a third-date conversation should be. This isn't even half the conversation to be had. We haven't even discussed my weight or, you know, past relationships that tanked badly. It seems like the baggage quotient in dating me is super high."

"Girl, you are worth it. You are worth all the baggage and more. Keep your head up. If he doesn't text you back, I'd be shocked and mad at him. You are worth all of him and more."

"Thanks, Jessie. You are a true friend and angel."

"Did I tell you I have a date tonight? I guess one of the speed-dating people really liked me, but it took his time to get the courage to reach out. So here I am, getting ready for a night out, wondering if I even remember this dude. That wine, that night, went down smooth."

Nika giggled. "The wine was terrible, Jessie!"

"And in spite of that, it still went down smooth." Jessie retorted.

"Good luck!"

"I'll need it!"

"Hey, at least he won't email you telling you that you need a personal trainer in order to be seen in public with him."

"Oh god, that was the worst. I can't believe someone would DO that to you."

Nika smiled, put her phone on the coffee table, grabbed her warm mug of coffee, and decided to finally watch the finale of that Viking show she really liked. Nothing like half-naked men hacking each other to death to remind her of the better things in life.

About an hour later, her phone vibrated again.

She picked it up, assuming it was Jessie, but when she saw the green message saying "Jason," she hesitated. She wasn't sure if she was ready for a letdown.

Finally, after staring at it for 5 minutes, she opened up the messages.

"Hey! I just wanted to say that I really enjoyed your company, and I'm sorry if I made you feel that things weren't so great last night. I want to see you again, maybe talk some more, and just make sure you are okay. Can we do that?"

She smiled softly as she texted back. "Sure, want to watch a movie at my place?"

"Yes! We can do that. Give me your address and let me know what snacks you like. I'll bring some stuff over. Do you want wine or beer?"

"Actually, I have some really good rum here. Want to grab some cokes for me, some popcorn, and I'll make caramel corn and have rum and cokes."

"Sounds great. I'll bring double and have the same."

She gave him her address, and they committed to having him come over at about 7 pm that evening.

She looked around her place and decided to clean up a bit. Maybe freshen up a little too. After all, PJs may give him a completely different idea tonight. She wasn't too ready for a Netflix and chill moment just yet.

While cleaning up, she debated putting away the various indigenous catalogs and items she had out. Angrily, she told herself to stop whitewashing who she was just because she liked a guy. She decided if he couldn't live with it while they were dating, he sure wouldn't like it if they went any further, and she wasn't about to change. She couldn't, not for any man.

It felt like it both took a long time and yet no time at all for 7 pm to arrive. She found the time to text Jessie that Jason had reached out and was now coming over. She had a hot minute to meltdown about letting him into her space before Jessie's date arrived. When Jason finally rang the doorbell, she almost fell out of her chair. Taking a deep breath, she went to let him in.

She laughed as she let him in.

"What's so funny?"

"Oh, Jessie, she's wishing me luck while she's going on a first date with one of her speed-dating connections. It should be me wishing her luck. Come on in, make yourself at home while I send her a quick message back."

"Sure thing." He looks around curiously at her place, touching some things and staring at others. "Nice place." He nods while making his way to the kitchen at the back of the house.

She quickly texts Jessie to tell her good luck as well, then she looks up from her phone as he wanders through her space

"Thanks! Buying my own home and making it into a space that showcased my personality was the highlight of my late 20s," she laughed.

"You've got a really nice place here. Great colors and interesting art, but my place sadly looks like a bachelor pad. I don't think I have a single thing on the walls."

She laughed. "Priorities, right?"

"My mom keeps saying I need a woman's touch. Somehow, I think this is what she's talking about. Throw pillows and things on the walls. All along, I figured she meant a home-cooked meal, and I was offended because I'm a pretty good cook, if I say so myself!"

Nika laughed again. "I'm sure your place is just fine."

"Well, it's clean; it just has no personality."

He frowned, "I think I get points for it being clean."

"Yes, you do!"

"Where are your glasses? I'll make the drinks. Will you make the popcorn? I distinctly remember someone promising Caramel Corn."

"Here you go," she pointed to a cupboard where the glasses were, and pointed to the bottom freezer for ice. "The rum is over there." She pointed at a hutch that doubled as a bar.

She started cooking down the butter while she popped the popcorn in the microwave. About twenty minutes later, they had drinks in hand and soft, buttery, sweet caramel corn in a big bowl. They had fallen into that easy camaraderie they had discovered before those heavy conversations of Friday night. Laughter and jokes, easy ribbing, it felt good.

"What do you want to watch? I'm up for something fun and mindless."

"Nic Cage or Tom Cruise?"

She stops and stares at him. "Seriously? Do they even act anymore?"

He stops and covers his heart as if suffering a heart attack. "Do they even act anymore?! Don't you attack my bros!"

She laughs uproariously. "Oh, you are a super fan. I get it, I get it. How about some Jason Momoa or Vin Diesel?"

He clutches his heart even harder. "Oh, you're killing me, smalls! I can't compete against those beefcakes!"

She grins from ear to ear, "Oh, I'm sure you probably can."

He grins and leans in to quickly kiss the tip of her nose. "I'm so flattered you think so."

She freezes and stares at him with a surprised look on her face while her face blushes.

"Too soon?" He asks.

She stutters out. "No... No. Just unexpected. Nice but unexpected. I wasn't ready for that." She can feel herself starting to babble.

His voice deepens as he moves in closer. "I've been wanting to do that for a few days now. Been thinking about it and this too." he leans in and kisses her long and slow on the mouth. She leans into him with a soft, small moan. His mouth is warm and soft, and his hand snakes around her to pull her into his warmth. As he pulls away from the kiss, he says, "Just as I thought, perfect."

She blushes harder as she lays her head on his chest. "Oh wow."

He pulls her face up to look at him with his finger under her chin and says, "Good, wow? or …"

"No good, good, very good, wow." She smiles at him.

"Good," he smiles back. "Now about Nic Cage."

She burst into peals of laughter. "Whatever you want. You pick it, and I'll watch whatever you want."

Jason picks something action-packed and sits down on the couch. She sits down beside him, and he wraps his arm around her shoulders. He pulls her into his chest while he presses play. They both get comfortable as she snuggles in. "You good?" he asks. "I'm fantastic," she replies.

They snuggle and watch for about 45 minutes. Crunching on the popcorn and sipping their drinks.

Suddenly, he leans down and says in her ear. "I'm sure this movie is fascinating, but all I can think about right now is kissing you. I'm going to turn you towards me in about two seconds and kiss you unless you tell me you don't want to."

She turns to face him, tipping her head up to give him access to her lips. "Is one second okay?"

He growls as he lowers his head down to claim her lips.

She lost track of time as his lips covered hers, kissing her passionately.

Suddenly, she felt him pick her up and turn her to face him, putting her down in his lap and straddling him. She pulled away slightly to look at him.

He looked into her eyes and said, "Don't stop now. I was just getting to the fun part." He had a happy smile on his face, his eyes intense with need.

"Okay," she said softly, leaning in for more, her hands gripping the sides of his face to bring him closer.

His hands wound themselves around her body, pulling her close, gripping her bottom to rub her against him. He was so hard. So hard and so hot. It made her feel needy and breathy.

She leaned in close and kissed him softly. Feeling him groan into her mouth, she deepened the kiss. He kissed her back and swept his tongue into her mouth.

She pulled away to catch her breath.

He whispered, "Oh fuck" grabbed her neck, and pulled her in deep, making the kiss hot, ferocious, and all-consuming. She moaned and rubbed up against him.

They kissed like that for what felt like ages. Finally, he pulled away and said, "Nika, honey, are we doing this? Because I don't want to stop, not one little bit." he pulled her in and pressed his forehead against hers while taking a deep breath. "Whew. I don't think I can stop. I mean, I can, but I'll be really, really uncomfortable for a while."

Nika giggled into his chest, took a deep breath, and looked up at him. "Come on, let's go to my bedroom." He stilled. "You sure?"

She had a small attack of insecurity. "Well, I mean, if you don't want to, I completely understand."

"Oh Jesus, no, woman, I very much want to. I just need to make sure this is what you want. No doubt, just this."

"Oh. No. No doubt, just this." She climbed off his lap and stood up shakily. She reached out for his hand and turned her head at the stairs. "Come on, let's go upstairs and see where this takes us."

He got up, and she walked them to the stairs, where he suddenly grabbed her and wrapped her legs around his waist. She pulled her in for a quick kiss and then started climbing up the stairs. Caught off guard, she grabbed his shoulders.

"Jason! I'm too heavy! Put me down!"

"You're perfect. Just direct me so I don't end up in the bathroom or the craft room or whatever you have up there." He grabbed her ass and squeezed. "Kiss me," He ordered as they made their way up the stairs.

She kissed him passionately, and he staggered a little bit. She raised her head. "No, I'm good, I'm good. You just taste so god damned good." He reached the top of the stairs. "Where am I going?"

"Second door on the right." She was feeling so hot that she hoped he would get there soon.

He opened the door to a large bedroom with a king-sized bed. He grinned at her and said, "Like 'em big, huh?"

"What!?" She blushed furiously.

He gestured to the bed.

"Oh, I'm not the best sleeper, and I end up all over the place. After I fell out of bed, a queen, by the way, in college, I decided that the first big purchase I made was going to be a king big enough for me to toss and turn in. I present to you my one and only King in my life."

"I'm kinda hoping to change that for you."

"Wait, are you saying?" She blushed hard. "I mean, it's been a while, I'm not sure I have any …. thing you know like lube…to help you along if…. I'm no size queen."

"What?" He snorted and laughed. "NO, I meant I would treat you like a queen, but I would like to add that I've never gotten any complaints from that department." He leaned in and kissed her fiercely to distract her from the discussion.

She returned the kiss and wrapped her arms around him again. Her nails, like daggers digging into his back, just spurred him on to make the kisses deeper and stronger.

He walked them both towards the bed and slowly leaned over until her back touched the mattress. Putting a hand beside her head, he brought a knee up and leaned down and into her, placing his weight on her as he deepened the kiss.

She tangled her hands into his hair, not wanting to let go. Moaning softly, she opened her legs, letting the weight of him cradle against her hip. Lord, help her. He was so hot and heavy, and it had been so long that she felt so good.

He pulled back a bit and tugged his sweater off. She took the hint and leaned up on her elbows to start unbuttoning her shirt. She stopped mid-button to stare at his chest. He looked big with clothes on, but somehow, when he took his shirt off, he looked massive. The long winding tattoo ran up his left arm, then over one pectoral. His abs were peeking out as he hunched over her.

"Holy shit. WOW. Uhm…"

"Here, hon, lemme help you with that." His gentle fingers took over unbuttoning her shirt, and with a soft sigh of pleasure, he opened up her shirt to reveal her curves. He ran his hands over her skin. She arched into him and sighed. "Please don't stop."

"I don't intend to."

His thumbs slipped under her sports bra, and he pulled it up and over her head. Her heavy breasts fell onto her chest and into his hands. "Oh dear lord, that's good."

She blushed as he squeezed them and ran the nipples between his forefinger and his thumb. She arched into him again.

"Atta girl, you like that, don't you?"

She nodded her head and stretched out like a cat. He took the invitation and squeezed a little harder, then dipped his head down to take a nipple into his hot, waiting mouth. She gasped with pleasure and simultaneously arched into his mouth while her hand came up behind him to grip his hair.

"Oh, Jason," she moaned, "Don't stop."

He pushed his thigh higher up, rubbing it against her core, making her feel crazy with heat and need.

"Jason, I'm going to need you to speed up or slow down soon. I'm getting too close too fast."

"It's okay, baby, just ride it. I got you."

His hands settled around her sweatpants, and he started tugging them down. He pulled them off her feet and then came back to rub against her, the fabric of his jeans driving her crazy as she was so sensitive and wet down there.

She started thrashing her head frantically, moaning softly.

"Come on, baby, just let it go. I got you. Just let it go." He slipped a thick finger inside of her. "Oh, lord, you are so wet, so perfect." She just about came off the bed. He grabbed her hands and put them over her head, holding her down as he nibbled on her nipples and slowly thrust his finger inside of her, his thumb rubbing her clit.

"Atta girl, you're so close. You're gonna explode for me soon, aren't you? Just let it happen."

He leaned in for a hot, fiery kiss as he pushed two fingers into her. She half moaned and screamed into his mouth, her hips bucking a bit, pushing him in deeper. He put more pressure on his thumb while it moved in circles on her clit.

"Come on, baby, come for me. Let me take care of you first. I promise we'll get there together, but you just need to take this right now. You can do it. I'm going to put another finger in now, and I'm going to give your nipple a little bite right here," he kissed the tip of her nipple, "and then you will come all over my hand, won't you, baby."

She moaned and arched again.

He leaned in really close to her ear and said, "Remember what I told you? I'm going to bite, and you're going to cum all over my hand."

He kissed his way down to her breast, laved it with his tongue, and then gave it a sharp, small bite while pushing into her with three fingers. She screamed and started bucking, and he could feel her coming all over his fingers, squeezing his fingers tightly.

"Atta girl."

He moved his fingers lazily in and out while his other hand let go of her arms to adjust his straining hardness.

"I'm sorry."

"For what? That was magnificent."

"But you didn't. We didn't."

"Oh, honey, we are going right now. Trust me, I'm not even remotely close to done."

He leaned in close and kissed her softly. "I just have to get you all excited all over again."

He stood up, leaving her cold on the bed as he unbuttoned his jeans. She blushed at the wet spot on the top of his thigh.

He looked down at it and then at her reddened face. "I don't think I'm ever going to wash these. That was hot."

She blushed harder and straightened her legs, closing her thighs a bit.

"Uh uh uh," he gripped her thighs and pushed them slightly open. "Trust me, I'm enjoying the view. You keep them right there."

He bent over to pull his legs out of his jeans, his nose just about at her core. He leaned in and licked a long, slow lick, and she just about came off the bed. He chuckled. "This time, I'm going to need you to slow down a bit, honey."

"Then stop doing that!" She gasped, her body thrumming from the sensitivity.

"I don't think I can," he grinned.

He started rummaging through his jeans and then pulled out some condoms.

"I'm on birth control, by the way," she said.

"Hey, let me look after you. I'm 100% sure I'm okay, and I'm almost 100% sure you are okay, but we're still learning from each other, and I want to take care of you. I want you to feel safe and know that I'm going to look after us," he stared seriously into her eyes.

She shook her head in agreement, a warm feeling of attraction just washing over her. "Thank you, I like that."

"Plus, I'll last longer," he grinned devilishly.

"I'm not worried about how long you'll last this time!" She retorted.

He laughed. "Oh baby, you're so hot you're practically on fire, so I'm worried about me."

He stroked her hip, slowly moving up to squeeze a breast, and then lay out beside her. Touching and stroking her in places, working her back up to a frenzied, aroused state.

It didn't take her long to get all worked up again. Moaning and calling his name out, she frantically grabbed at his hair and pulled him in for a deep kiss. He took the opportunity to lean in, pushing her thighs wide apart while he slowly sank into her. She gasped into his mouth. He pulled away from her and groaned. "God, so wet and so tight. Heaven couldn't be better than this."

"Maybe I should be a size queen," she gasped out. "It feels almost too tight."

"Don't worry, baby, I'll go slow till you're there with me." He pulled out slowly and sank back in, pushing even further.

She scratched her nails down his back while she hooked her legs around his waist, pulling him in deeper. Arching up to meet him, she groaned; it felt so good.

"Please don't stop, please." She repeated over and over.

"Don't worry, Nika baby. I don't think I can stop for anything right now." He hurried the pace, pulling up and sinking deep with each hard thrust. She could see a sheen of sweat building up on his forehead as he fought the urge to start slamming into her. She opened herself wider, bit her lip, and said, "Jason, don't hold back. Let yourself go this time."

He looked at her questioningly, "Are you sure? I want you to really love this. I want to do this over and over and over."

"Trust me, just let go. I got you, babe." She repeated his words back to him as she felt him brace himself up on his elbows, digging them into the mattress on either side of her. He started to piston in and out of her, slamming himself into her. His eyes were wide with that intense concentration. She raised her hips up to meet him thrust for thrust, reveling in the feeling of him pushing into her. "Oh, Jason, I'm so close again. Please come, please," she whispered in a soft, strained voice.

"Oh fucking hell." He felt his whole body tense up, and everything just peaked and let go. He thrust hard against her, grinding himself deep into her while he groaned and collapsed on top of her.

It didn't take long before she felt him chuckling as he wrapped his arms around her and rolled onto his side, bringing her with him.

"God, that was perfect."

She stroked her hands along his chest, "Was it really?"

He jerked his head up and looked at her incredulously, "You didn't think so?"

"No, no, it was amazing for me, but it's just been so long, and I wasn't sure if it was that good for you."

"Oh no, no, no. You don't get to think that. That was perfect. That exceeded all my expectations. Give me about 20 minutes, and I'll show you again how wonderful I thought that was."

She laughed and moaned, "I need more than 20 minutes! I'm going to hurt in places I didn't even know I had!"

"Oh, I'll show you hurt." He grinned lecherously.

Suddenly, his stomach grumbled.

She laughed. "Hungry? Wanna grab supper?"

Chapter 8

She got up from the bed and grabbed his hand. "Come on," she said, shyly leading him to the shower in her ensuite bathroom. "Let's clean up, and then we'll grab a bite. Do you have anywhere you need to be tonight?"

"I do not. I'm all yours."

She flushed with pleasure. "I like that."

They climbed into the shower and laughed while they washed each other, talking about random things while they soaped up. Then, suddenly, they were kissing again, and she moaned and pulled away. "I can't go again just yet. I need some time."

"It's good, babe. Let's order some pizza and maybe try watching something again."

They toweled off while they discussed pizza toppings, quickly realizing that it was one area they wouldn't always agree on. He wanted it hot and spicy, while she preferred simple and classic. He grabbed his phone and started ordering from the app while she threw on her shirt and panties. She was looking around for her sweats when he looked up and said, "Just wear that. I've got a hankering for watching you walk around in nothing but that."

She blushed, "But I'll get cold!"

"That's what I'm here for, don't worry, you won't have a moment to get cold."

"We aren't going to last very long before we are back up here again, are we?"

"You gotta roommate?"

She frowned. "No, why?"

"Well then, who says we'll end up back here? That couch looks pretty comfy with a good spring to it."

She laughed, "Oh, I see how it is. Are you claiming every inch of my house?"

"Nope, just you."

"I could be up for that."

"That's what I was hoping to hear."

They wandered downstairs, and she slipped onto the couch under a blanket, where he grabbed them another drink. When the doorbell rang with the pizza, he ordered her to stay on the couch while he picked it up. She could see him and her getting really comfortable with his presence in the house. He just seemed to fit there. He put the pizzas down on the coffee table and looked up at her.

"What?" he asked. She smiled and said, "I was just thinking that you fit in here. I like you being here, in my house with me."

He smiled back. "I like it too. Let me get some plates and napkins."

"Top left cupboard and then in the bottom right drawer!" she called out while he ambled back into the kitchen.

He came back with the plates and napkins, and they fell into the pizza in companionable silence. They start the movie that was interrupted earlier.

Once they were done with the pizza, he pulled her into his lap, and they watched the last 20 minutes of the movie with her in his lap, his one hand playing with her hair while his other rubbed her inner thigh. They made it through the credits, and she turned to look at him, "So, this is where it gets awkward."

"Oh? How so?"

"Well, uhm. Are you staying? Going? Is this it for tonight? Or are you up for breakfast tomorrow morning?"

He gripped her chin and pulled her in for a kiss. "I told you I was yours tonight. I'm here all night. I could ask you to tour your bedroom, but I already know how to get there. Want to head up there for the night?"

"Yes, please."

"Please!" He laughed, "You are so cute and polite. What do we need to do to shut the place down?"

"Make sure the front and back doors are locked, turn off the TV, make sure all the food is put away, and then we're done."

He frowned. "No alarm system?"

She sighed. "You sound like my mom, but no, I haven't had time to get that installed."

He kissed her forehead. "Oh, well, I'm here tonight. But maybe next weekend, I'll install that."

"You don't have to do that." She insisted. "No," he said emphatically, "I don't think we're ready for me to be here every night, and until that is installed, I will either be here, or I will worry about you. So it's going in, it's done."

"OK then, if it's for your peace of mind."

"It's definitely for my peace of mind."

"Well, I can't argue that, but just, you know, know it's not your job to look after me."

"It is now, honey," He stops Nika at the foot of the stairs before they go upstairs. "Look, we're lovers now. Everything feels really good, and I really like you. I don't see this ending anytime soon; if anything, we'll likely get more serious. Let me look after you, take care of you, and show you how I feel about you, OK? You aren't taking advantage, and I'm not infringing on your independence. We'll take this as slow as you need, but I also need to show you how I feel, and for me, that means doing things for you to feel good about how I treat you and how I take care of you."

She swallowed heavily and nodded, tears forming in her eyes. "It's a lot and fast, Jason, but I like you too, and I understand. I won't argue too much, but I will put in a token effort to remind you that you don't have to, and I can take care of myself."

"It's all good, babe. Let's go to bed."

He grabbed her hand and pulled her up the stairs, where they made love, then fell asleep in a tangle of limbs.

Chapter 9

The next morning, they laughed over eggs and bacon. She was shocked at how much Jason could pack away, watching him eat almost all the bacon, 4 eggs, and then the rest of the pizza.

She teased him about wearing him out last night.

He shook his head. "Nah, babe, I'm carb-loading. I got a big lift this afternoon at the gym, and I need all the oomph I can get, which reminds me, can I get another cup of coffee?"

"Big lift? What's that?"

"I lift weights, hon. It's my self-care. I hit the gym and push the iron. If you want to come with me sometime, I'd welcome that. Even if just to watch me and cheer."

Nika bit her lip; she and the gym had never been friends. He read her hesitancy.

"I'm not trying to change you. I love you as you are, but I would love the company. I just like being around you."

She nodded, "Not today. I have to get ready for Monday tomorrow, so I'm not prepared today, but maybe someday, OK?"

"Sure thing, babe."

"So…...how much do you...you know...what's it called? Bench?"

"Did you just look that up on your phone?"

"Mayyyyyyyybe."

He laughs, "God, you are cute. My bench is a bit of poverty (meaning I struggle with it). It's a measly 250 pounds. You should have asked what my deadlift or squat is."

"250 pounds! That's more than I weigh!"

"I know! I lifted you! Very easily, I might add."

She blushed, remembering last night. Then, she took the bait. "OK, what are your squat and deadlift, and what's a deadlift anyway?"

"My squat is 375 right now. I put the bar on my shoulders and then squat down and come back up."

"Holy shit, that's…. that's a lot of weight."

"Trust me, I know." He grinned at her. She could tell he was really enjoying this conversation. "And my deadlift is one of pure beauty. I just broke a PR or PB of 400 lbs. on it. That's when you load the bar on the floor and just pick it up and put it down. Pure dead weight, hence deadlift."

"Four!" She held up four fingers. "Hundred. Pounds?!? What's a PR/PB?"

"Personal Record, or Personal Best. It's my current most successful attempt. I'm trying to get 405, but I just can't get it up completely."

"Isn't 400 enough?"

"Oh no, honey, this is my fun. I want to keep going till I can't go anymore. Getting stronger and stronger, lifting heavier and heavier." He leaned up against her kitchen counter, his arms crossed, and grinned at her.

"That's why I would love to have you come with me sometime. My girl and my favorite activity would be my heaven."

She blushed to hear him say, My girl. "OK then, I'll come, but not today. I have things to do. But I will make a point of coming with you at some point. Promise."

"That's all I can ask for. And with that, I gotta go." He leans in for a quick kiss. "See you later, Princess. Have a good week, and I'll text you."

"You too, handsome!"

Chapter 10

She texted Jessie as soon as he left.

"Hey, are we still shopping? I have some groceries I need to pick up, as Jason just about ate me out of the house and home, and then I want to get a new sweater for the office. Someone's turned the heat down to positively arctic temperatures. How did your date go?"

"Yes! I have so much to tell you. I had a great time, and wait, wait, WAIT. Jason did what? How was it when you let him into your personal space? How was it? Did you guys watch a movie? DEETS, I need deets!"

"He may have come over last night, and we ordered pizza and watched a movie."

"How is that eating you out of the house and home if he brought pizza?"

"He didn't bring it; we ordered it, and it wasn't the pizza. It was the eggs and bacon this morning."

She grinned, waiting for the phone to blow up.

"HE STAYED THE NIGHT?! Stay right where you are. I'm hopping in my car right now, and I'll be there in record time!"

Nika grinned foolishly and went upstairs to finish getting ready. She slapped on some quick foundation and eyeliner, then put on jeans and a warm sweater for shopping.

By the time she was dressed, Jessie was in her driveway waiting.

She locked the door, straightened the planter on her front porch table, it looked like someone had pushed it over. Perhaps it was windy last night. She thought as she slowly made her way to Jessie's car. As she opened the door, Jessie blasted her, "You better start talking fast. I need to know everything."

"Well, he has a tattoo all up one arm and over his pec."

Jessie swooned. "You know I love tattoos."

"Apparently, I do, too. When he took off his shirt, and I saw it, I swear my eyes crossed, I got so aroused. Who would think that was my thing?"

"Andddddddddd…. how was it?"

"Colorful."

"NOT THE TATTOO. SEX!? My god, you are worse than my nieces at divulging information."

Nika laughed. "OK, it was amazing, all of it, every time, amazing and wonderful, and I think I am falling way too fast and way too hard for this guy."

"No way, not a thing," Jessie exclaimed. "I met him. He's like perfect, and the two of you looked perfect together."

"I appreciate your vote of confidence. I told him I took birth control, and he insisted on wearing a condom. He was like, It's my job to protect you. He kept saying that he liked me and that it was his job to make sure I was OK. He is going to install a security system in my house, and oh my god….Am I crazy?"

"Wow, he sounds…really nice. Like really caring and nice. He likes you."

"How was your supper?" Nika needed to change the subject while she thought about things.

"It was good. No sparks, but we will see. He's funny and warm, but also divorced, and I'm not sure I want to take on that baggage. He has a kid. Again, more baggage. It's a shame because otherwise, I had a great time. But I don't want to become another one of those lifetime movies full of angst, yelling, and finding common ground among damaged people. But I think I will have a few more dates with him and see where it goes." She sighs. "We're at that age, you know? I led with my career, and I'm happy with that, but I'm also aware that almost any man we meet at this point will have baggage, either a failed relationship or a divorce, and that's daunting. I mean, I have my baggage, too, but they will never have to meet my exes or deal with their issues. They just have to deal with me and my issues as a result of failed relationships. Which is enough."

Nika shook her head in agreement. "Which is enough. Although, if you guys get serious, he does have a good chance of meeting one of your exes."

Jessie burst out laughing. "OK, you have me there, but only during family reunions, weddings, and funerals. I still don't know why my cousin wanted to marry my ex. Like, couldn't you find your own loser to marry? But they are still married. It's been 7 years, and they seem happy. Maybe he grew up, but when I dated him, he had a loooong way to go. Did I tell you she was expecting? He's going to be a dad. I just," she shook her head, "he's going to be a dad, and I can't find Mr. Right. Maybe I am overthinking this too much."

Nika leaned over and half-hugged her. "Look, you are a great person, and you had dreams and goals that needed time and your focus. Getting married right out of high school or soon after wasn't an item on your bucket list, but it was on theirs. Just because you waited doesn't mean there aren't great options out there. There is someone for you. Maybe you will have to compromise on a few things, but hey, you would have had to compromise on a few things had you found Mr. Right 10 years ago. Maybe this guy will be the One, maybe he won't, maybe you will just enjoy a few dinners and then go your separate ways. I don't think anyone's keeping score, no matter how pressured we feel that the time is ticking."

Jessie laid her head on Nika's shoulder. "You are right. I just feel worried. What if time passes by and I never do everything I wanted to do?"

"You will. You are driven and determined. If anyone will make it happen, it will be you. Just don't drive yourself crazy over it. Here, let's change the subject. Did you know Jason lifts weights? He's benching 250, squatting 375, and deadlifting 400? Like, I don't know why I was worried when he lifted me and carried me up the stairs to bed."

"HE DID WHAT? HE DOES WHAT? Oh, I gotta sit down for a moment. Did you just find the golden unicorn of men, and you don't even know what you have?"

"What do you know about lifting weights?"

"My older brother does it, remember? He has that grimy hole of a gym where he and all his gym bros go and do their workouts, and then they all go home and eat tons of chicken and broccoli….and rice. Can't forget the rice." She rolled her eyes. "Anyways, he carried you up the stairs? He's pulling out all the stops. No man will ever compare to him."

"Well, then, I guess I better make sure there isn't a man after him." Nika paused. "Did I just say that?"

"Out of the mouth of babes. Oh, you're hooked, honey."

Nika nodded her head. "I am hooked."

She felt her phone vibrate, and she pulled it out of her jacket. It was a text from Jason with a video attached.

She sat down on a small bench with Jessie beside her. "Want to watch?"

Jessie laughed, "What if it's naughty?"

"I think it's a gym video."

"Oh yes, let's watch then."

Nika pressed play. Jason filled the screen. "Hey babe, I'm going to try for 405 here, and I thought I would film it for you to get an idea of what would happen when you come to the gym with me," he grinned. "Of course, I'm only hitting send on this if I'm successful, so here goes 405."

He put the phone down against something and walked over to a bar loaded with weights waiting on a rubber mat. He placed his feet squarely apart and leaned over to grab the bar. Then he took a couple of deep breaths and started pulling, his face instantly serious and turning red as the bar slowly climbed up his legs. He pulled it up to his waist and leaned back a bit, then put it down with a large slam.

He shouted out a loud "Hoo Boy! YES!" and then walked over to stop the video. Nika just turned and looked at Jessie.

Jessie mouthed, "Wow." Then, "So you are going to the gym?"

"Well, yes, he wants my company. He said I don't have to work out if I don't want to. He likes me the way I am, and he's not trying to change me, but he wants my companionship while he's working out, and he wants to show me things that excite him, and this clearly excites him."

"That excited ME, Nika. That's it. I have to find myself one of these men."

Nika laughs. "I wasn't looking for him! He fell in my lap!"

"Yes, but clearly, I will have to "look for him." That's OK, I can do this. I can find another one like him, with a few differences. By the way, that tattoo is hot."

"You think so too?"

They spent the rest of the afternoon chatting about work, clothes, and their next get-together.

Nika went home at the end of the long day with a large smile on her face. As she was unlocking the front door, juggling everything she had bought in her hands, she noticed her planter was off to the side of the little porch table.

Thinking nothing of it, she put her groceries in the hallway entrance and went back to straighten them out. She could have sworn the planter was pink and purple violets, but maybe she had picked red and orange Impatiens this summer. She could've sworn it was pink and purple.

She shrugged and went into the house. It took her about an hour to unload the groceries and put them away, then she made a quick dinner and started to wind down for bed. At about 9:30, Jason texted her.

"Hey, princess, just checking in. How was your afternoon?"

"Hey, handsome, it was great. Jessie and I had a good time shopping, and I got a few new pieces for the office. A nice warm sweater and some slacks. That video you sent me was amazing. I can't even think of lifting that much, but congratulations! You got 405! Maybe I'll make you a cake next time you are here."

"You know the way to my heart. Thank you. It was a bit of a grind, but I got it up. I think you were the magic equation that gave me the oomph to accomplish that."

"Aww, you are too sweet. Anyway, I must get to bed. See you soon?"

"Can't wait."

Chapter 11

Nika's days in the office passed without much incident. There was a bit of an odd day when a letter with her name on it was dropped off at her office, but within it was a request for her personal accounting services. Sometimes, if someone admired their corporate work, they would request that they do their personal taxes, too. She sent the inquiry a nice letter declining the work, and that was the end of that as far as she was concerned.

Jason and she texted every night in the evening to get to know each other better. She agreed that this weekend, she would go to the gym with him, and while it gave her some anxiety, Jason was doing his best to calm her down. She worried that she wouldn't fit in or would be made fun of for being curvier than most people in the gym. Jason promised her that his gym wasn't like that. She really hoped he was right.

They decided to go out for dinner on Friday. Jason would spend the night, and then, on Saturday, they would go to the gym together. Sunday, if they were still getting along, would be spent lazing around the house.

On Thursday, she came home to a beautiful bouquet of roses on her front step. Her neighbor texted her that someone had dropped them off at about 2 pm, and she kept an eye on them to make sure no one took off with them. Nika inhaled the blooms and smiled. What an absolutely beautiful thing. The card said, "I look forward to spending more time with you."

She picked up her phone and texted Jason, "I'm looking forward to spending more time with you, too!"

"Aww, thanks! Where did that come from?"

"Oh, I'm just admiring the roses you sent me. Thank you! They are beautiful."

"I didn't send you any roses."

"Oh, Jason, I didn't take you for a jokester. They were waiting for me on the front porch this afternoon. The card says, 'I'm looking forward to spending more time with you.' Who else would they be from? It's silly!"

"I don't know, but they didn't come from me."

Nika's smile slowly faded from her face.

"You're serious, are you?"

"Serious as a heart attack, darling. You aren't/weren't talking to anyone else, were you?"

"NO."

"OK, OK, I had to ask. Why don't I come over and we talk about this?"

"If you want to."

"Be right there, babe."

Chapter 12

When Jason came to the house, he found her looking pale and upset. He hugged her close. "It'll be OK; we'll figure this out."

"I texted all my friends to see who may have played a prank like this, but none of them knew what was going on. I don't like this, Jason!"

"You don't recognize the writing on the card?"

"No, do you?" She hands him the card. He studies it intently, "Nah. This is really bothering you?"

"Jason, I haven't had a date in over a year. You are the first in a long time, and none of them have gotten far enough to know where I live. I don't know who could have done this."

"Wow," he paused and thought for a minute. "I didn't realize it had been that long for you. Yeah, that changes things. Look, I'll stay here tonight. I'll get up early and leave so I can change before work. But I'll stay and make sure you are safe. I picked up a security alarm, and I actually have it in the truck. I'll go get it and my tools, and I'll set that up tonight. We'll work to make you as safe as we can. OK?"

"OK. I don't like feeling like this. I feel really powerless."

He pulled her in for a hug and kissed her forehead. "We'll make you feel safe again, babe."

He picked her up, put her on the couch, and draped a blanket over her. "Look, I'll just run out to the truck and grab the stuff. Then I'll be right back, I promise."

He ran out quickly to his truck. Unbeknownst to him, he was being watched. He brought in the tools and the security system.

The man in his car, two houses down, angrily watched her house. This wasn't supposed to work this way! Of course, this stupid jock would take credit for HIS flowers. Of course, this slut would believe him. How dare they! Well, he would not be ignored. She would pay for letting this guy touch her, and she would pay for this disrespect! But what should he have expected from a girl like her? Girls like her never appreciate a real man like him.

Jason got to work. It had been a while since he had installed anything of this caliber, so he sauntered over to Nika and sat down. "I know you aren't feeling very good right now, but I want to install this right, and I could really use a friend's help. I want to call Cal and see if he can help me, but I don't want you to feel violated by having a stranger in your home. Do you want to call Jessie and see if she can come over and distract you with some conversation?"

"I don't know. Do you really need his help?"

"Well, I could try and muddle through, but then we run the risk of it not working properly, and I think that wouldn't be the most peaceful moment for you or for me."

"That makes sense, call Cal, and I'll text Jessie."

She grabbed her phone, her fingers still slightly shaking. "Hey, can you come over? I'm having a bit of a day, and Jason suggested that you come over. I'll explain when you come here if you don't mind."

"I'll be right there. Are you OK?"

"I will be."

Nika looked up at Jason, "Jessie's on her way."

"So is Cal. Look, Cal is super nice, if a bit shy. Not much of a talker, more the quiet type."

"Quieter than you?"

Jason barked out a short laugh. "Yep. Amazingly enough."

"Where did you meet him? Do you work together?"

"Not really, sometimes we use him as a consultant on big projects we have at work, but mostly, we work out at the same gym together. He's an electrician and has helped me out with some electrical work in my own place also, so he was the first guy I thought of when I knew this was more complex than I had thought."

"Oh, cool." The front door rang, and Jason went to get the door. Jessie rushed in as he opened the door. "What happened!?"

Jason grinned. "Hey, Jessie. Nice to see you, too."

Nika laughed. Jessie really could be a firework when she wanted to be. "Come to the kitchen, and I'll pour you some wine and show you."

As they walked into the kitchen, Jessie shouted. "Holy crap, look at those flowers! Nice work, Jason!"

He heard Nika say, "He didn't send them."

"What? Pour that wine and tell me all about it."

"Well, there's not much to tell. I came home to them on my front porch. They were delivered at about 2 pm, according to my neighbor. The card with them says, 'Looking forward to spending more time with you,' But Jason didn't send them, and none of my exes know where I live."

"OK, that's creepy. Really creepy. So what are we doing about it? Can we trace who ordered them?"

Nika shook her head, "No florist information. The card was a generic Safeway florist card. The neighbor said it was delivered by a slim man in a ball cap with a regular car, and there was no florist information or logo on the car at all."

"Oh, creepier and creepier."

"Jason is installing a security system right now, which we talked about last weekend. His friend Cal is coming over to help him, and he suggested I get you to come over since I'm upset and about to let a strange man into my house."

"He really does think of everything, huh?"

"I really hope so." Jessie grabbed Nika's hands. "Oh, jeez, you are cold. Let's go turn on the fireplace and talk in there. She grabbed her wine glass and the bottle. Nodding her head in the living room. "Come on, Nika."

The doorbell rang as they sat down. Jason called out, "It's Cal, I got it." As he went for the door. They overheard him saying, "Thanks, man, for coming. I really appreciate it. My girlfriend had a bit of a scare this evening, and I'd really like to get this installed properly tonight."

"No problem, man," they heard a deep voice reply.

Jason led the way to the wall where he wanted to install the panel, all the while talking. "So I think this makes the most sense for the installation. What do you think?"

Cal dipped his head in assent and looked around the corner in the living room. He said a soft "Hey," and Jason turned around. "Oh yeah, my bad. Nika, this is Cal, the best guy you'll meet. He's going to help me with the installation. That blonde bombshell over there is Jessie, Nika's best friend. She came out for support."

Cal quietly said. "This is a good alarm system. It'll fix you right up. Jason knows where it's at. I'm sorry you had a scare today."

Jessie was still blushing over Jason's bombshell comment. It was rare to see her speechless. Cal looked at her and said, "Nice to meet you, Jessie, Nika's friend."

"Uh...yeah." Stammered Jessie. "Nice to meet you, too."

Nika turned her head to see what was wrong with her best friend. Jessie looked stunned.

"What's wrong?"

"He's beautiful! Jason called me a bombshell! Where do I start?"

Nika laughed and took a sip of her wine. "He lifts, you know. That's where Jason met him."

Jessie turned to stare at Nika. "He what?"

"He lifts." She frowns. "Am I matchmaking?"

"He's perfect. Do you think he's dating? All the good ones are dating."

Jason chose just that moment to walk by. "Need a wrench." He leans in close. "Nope, he's single, but he's shy. That's why he's single. Shy, quiet, needs a little kick in the pants, you know." He winks at Jessie.

"Oh, I can give him a kick in the pants, all right."

Nika howled with laughter. "You two are horrible! Horrible people!"

Cal walks in. "What's going on?" Nika laughed even harder. Jessie blushed and glared at Nika.

"We were just talking about the gym. Nika is thinking of going to watch Jason lift this weekend."

Cal nodded his head. "Ah, I see. Are you going to come too?"

Jessie fired back, "Only if you are going to be there." Then she slapped her hand over her mouth. "I mean, if Nika wants the support, sure."

Cal nodded his head again. "I'll be there. See you, Saturday Jessie."

He walked back over to the panel. Jessie and Jason stared at him in stunned silence. Finally, Jason muttered, "I've never seen him act like that before." He followed Cal to the panel.

Jessie whispered to Nika, "Pass that bottle. I need another glass. Mama just got herself a date with a god."

Nika laughed loudly again. She couldn't help herself.

Chapter 13

Jason promised to stop by early on Friday night and spend the evening with her. They would get up in the morning, have a lazy day on Saturday, and then head to the gym, where they would meet Cal and Jessie. Jason was still shaking his head over Cal from Thursday night. "I swear to god, Nika, I have never seen him act like that around a girl before. I didn't even have to talk Jessie up for him. He had a date with her so fast I thought my head was spinning."

Nika laughed. "Well, I can see it. She's beautiful, blonde, and happy. What more could a guy want?"

"Oh, I can think of several things." His eyes got intense, and his voice dropped low and slow as he sauntered over to her. They were quickly settling into a pizza and drinks on Friday evenings while in their sweats, and Jason's sweats looked admirable on him. Hanging low on his hips, his bare feet sticking out of them, was so sexy to her. It spoke of a comfort she didn't realize she was searching for in a relationship. Jason made her feel very comfortable. She raised her eyes to look at him, and the dark look in his eyes suddenly made her feel distinctly uncomfortable. "Jason," she said warningly, "what are you up to?"

He grinned that wicked grin that made her heart stop. "Oh, I thought I would just come over here and give you a nice warm hug."

He wrapped his arms around her, pulling her into his chest. She inhaled his musky male scent and relaxed into him; suddenly, she was in the air, and she shrieked. "Jason! What are you doing?" As he set her down on the countertop.

He placed each arm on either side of her, his hands gripping the edge of the counter, trapping her between his frame. "Having a snack."

He dipped his head in low and captured her lips for a long, slow kiss that stoked the fires of her desire.

She moaned, "Jason." She tore her mouth away as he nuzzled into her neck and started kissing and nipping his way down her neck and chest. "Jason, the pizza is going to arrive any minute."

He chuckled. "I want dessert first." He undid one of the buttons on her shirt and pulled it open to reveal her luscious breasts. He leaned down and took one in his mouth while he stared up at her with those wicked eyes of his. His tongue licking the nipple and then his teeth gently nipping, she gasped and automatically spread her legs.

"Jason, I can't think when you would do this."

"Do you need me to stop?" He nipped her again.

"Yes. No. No. Oh god, please don't stop."

He pushed his frame into her spread thighs and rubbed himself up against her, the fabric driving her wild.

Suddenly, the doorbell rang. It was like cold water dashed on her skin. Jason pulled away and growled at her. "Stay there like that. I'll get the pizza. But I want to come back to this picture and finish what we started." He stared at her as if trying to memorize her while he walked to the door to grab the pizza.

He opened the door to find a thin older man holding the pizzas. "Hey man, thanks for the pizza." Holding out a ten as a tip, he grabs the boxes. The older man doesn't let go, and Jason frowns, looking up at the guy. He was craning his neck, trying to see around Jason.

"Hey man, you gotta problem?" Jason flexed his arms and stepped into the doorframe, blocking the guy from viewing inside.

"Oh no, no, I'm just. For some reason, I thought a girl ordered the pizza."

"Why does that matter, man?" Jason was getting angry. Suddenly, the man noticed Jason's heated words.

"Oh, I'm sorry, I don't know what came over me. Here's your pizza, thanks for the tip." He backed up and walked down the porch steps.

He muttered angrily as he walked to his car. She was supposed to open the door, see him, and suddenly realize how wrong she had been to dismiss him. It wasn't supposed to be that man! He had gone through great efforts to see her. He had intervened with the young man walking to the house and tipped him a whole 5 dollars just to finish the delivery and see her at the door. It wasn't fair. This wasn't how it was supposed to go.

He slammed his car door as he got in and drove away angrily. He'll just have to try better next time.

Jason walked back into the kitchen with the pizza in his hand, confused by the interaction he had just had with the pizza delivery guy, but when he walked into the kitchen to see Nika perched on the countertop, her legs splayed, lips swollen from his kisses and her breasts with their tight nipples on display for him, the whole thing was forgotten. Tossing the pizza on the table, he grinned as he walked right up to her. He slowly dragged a finger up her arm and then cupped her breast with his now cold hand.

She gasped. "That took a while."

"Worth it, though." He dipped his head and licked her nipple with his hot, wet tongue. "Now, where were we?"

"I believe you said something about how you wanted dessert first?"

"I really do have the best ideas," Jason drawled as he cupped her bottom and raised her up enough to tug off her sweats.

"Jason!" Nika gasped breathlessly. "What are you doing?"

"Dessert, honey, I'm making dessert."

After he tugged her sweats down and off, he pushed her thighs wider, pushing her back on the countertops, then with a devilish grin, he started going down in a kneeling position.

"Oh, Jason, I don't think that..." She couldn't even finish her thought before his hot tongue was licking long, slow licks up and down her core. "Jason!" she called out breathlessly while throwing her head back.

He pulled away and looked up at her while slowly inserting a lone finger. Her head rolled around till her chin hit her chest. She looked into his eyes, her body all hot and her head swimming with intense feelings from his ministrations.

"Now, this is a beautiful, delicious dessert. I'm a lucky man."

She blushed and moaned as he pushed his finger slowly back into her. "Jason, don't stop, please."

"Don't worry, honey, I got you," as he dipped his head in for more.

Chapter 14

Nika stretched luxuriously in her bed and opened her eyes to see Jason leaning over her and kissing her forehead.

"Mornin' Princess"

"Morning, handsome. Thank you for last night."

"No, sweetheart, thank you."

He leaned in for a long, drugging kiss, then grabbed her and rolled her on top of him.

She shrieked in laughter. "Jason!"

"Yes, darling?" As he straddled her on top of him.

"I need to brush my teeth and have a cup of coffee. Do you want breakfast?"

"What's on the menu?" He grinned devilishly.

"Eggs and bacon and pancakes, you pervert. We have things to do. We have a gym date with Cal and Jessie, remember?"

He groaned. "Yeah, yeah, yeah."

"You shower, and I'll make breakfast, then I'll shower while you eat."

"I have a better idea. Why don't we shower together? Then I'll help you make breakfast." He rubbed her back with his strong hands.

Do we have time for a shower if we shower together? I have a feeling that things are going to get steamy with both of us in there.

"Oh, things will be steamy, all right." He winked.

"Oh, YOU!" she laughed as she rolled off him and walked into the hallway to get a towel for him from the linen closet.

"Fine, we'll shower together, but if we're late, I'm blaming you. I have no reservations about hanging you out to dry."

"I'm sure they will understand." he grabbed her and pulled her into the bathroom.

Their shower took twice as long as it should have, but she certainly felt relaxed and happy from all the attention Jason was giving her.

They stood in companionable silence as he did the eggs, and she made the pancakes, with the bacon crisping up in the oven.

She set the table as he put the food out, and they sat together with their cups of coffee, and she just smiled at him.

"Whaaaaat?" He asked.

"Nothing," she smiled wider. "I'm just happy."

He stabbed a couple of pancakes and put them on his plate. "I'm really glad. I'm very happy being with you, too."

"So, how long will your workout take?"

"About an hour and a half, two hours if I need the extra rest times."

"That long?"

"Yeah, but don't worry, Jessie will keep you company, and Cal and I will talk with you two while we're in between sets."

She nodded thoughtfully.

"Honey, it will be fine."

"No! I'm not worried. I know it will be fine, but in fact, you should be worried." She grinned mischievously.

"What me? Why?"

"What if I'm more impressed with Cal's lifting than yours?"

He sat back, stunned, then noticed the teasing glint in her eyes. "OH, you."

She laughed, relaxing as she sipped her coffee. "I'm just saying!"

Chapter 15

The gym was huge and chilly. The equipment was everywhere, and people were congregated in singles and doubles, working out in different places. She stuck close to Jason, holding his hand as they wandered towards the back. Suddenly, she felt his body stiffen as he called out, "Hey, Cal, those cages for us?"

She looked ahead to where Cal was, and she couldn't see any cages.

"Cages?" she asked.

"Yeah, those square steel frames are called Squat cages. We'll use them to set up our squats, and then we'll pull benches in to do our bench presses, and after, we'll move over to those mats," he pointed to the left of the cages, "and we'll finish up with our deadlifts and accessories over there."

"You and Cal work out together all the time?"

"Sometimes, particularly when attempting to achieve personal records (PRs), it is essential to spot each other in case of a failed lift. Reaching for a weight that has not been lifted before constitutes a PR."

"Fail a lift?"

"It happens, and sometimes you need a little help getting out of the hole. You'll see what I mean, or rather, hopefully you won't, but you'll get it. Don't worry. Soon, you will be old hat at this," he kissed the top of her head.

He dumps his gear on the bench beside the rack and starts taking off his jacket. Nika looks at Cal. "Jessie here?"

"Uh yeah, she's right behind you. She was in the bathroom."

Nika turns around, and Jessie gives her a big hug. "Cal and I drove here this morning. We went out last night and had a blast. I'm actually surprised I'm not hungover!" She looked over Nika's shoulder at Cal with a mischievous grin. "Jessie!" Nika laughed, "You sure do work fast!"

Jessie gave her a stubborn look. "I know what I want."

Cal got a quiet, goofy grin and stared at the floor while Jason smacked him on the shoulder.

"Things good, man?"

"Yeah, everything's great."

"OK then. I was thinking I would start with squats. What do you want to start with?" Jason asked.

"I want to start with the bench. Actually, I want to try out for that 255, and if I gas out on squats, I won't have it in the tank for that." Jason nodded, "Sounds good. I'll spot you for sure."

"Thanks, man."

Nika and Jessie pulled up an empty bench and sat down to watch and chat.

"Soooo," Nika starts, "How was your evening? I didn't know you and Cal were going out last night."

"It kind of happened. I gave him my number on Thursday to coordinate today, and when he texted me yesterday afternoon, he asked if I wanted to have dinner with him, and I just couldn't refuse."

"Must have been a good time."

"Oh, the BEST time," she grinned. "We just haven't stopped finding things to talk about, and before we knew it, we had closed down the restaurant. We went from there to a late-night bowling place, where we closed it down. Then we went back to my place and kept talking most of the night. "

"Talking, huh?" Nika grinned wickedly

"YES. Talking! Jeez Nika, some people like to talk to me, you know."

Cal grunted, and they both looked up to see him pushing what looked like a lot of weight on the bench.

"Jason?" Nika called out, "Don't you have to spot him?"

Jason laughed and shook his head. "He's just warming up. He's fine."

Jessie leaned over, "Nika, that's just 225. Cal can do that in his sleep."

"This is all just crazy to me! I know you are used to it because your brother used to lift weights like this, but they are lifting weights that weigh more than us, like it's nothing."

"I know, right? Isn't it just dreamy?"

"Well, I have to tell you, when Jason picks me up like I'm nothing, I'm pretty happy."

This time, it was Jessie's turn. "Oh, just happy, huh?"

"I said what I said!" They both tore out in laughter.

The rest of the afternoon was full of banter and laughter. A few of the guys who lifted routinely with Jason and Cal came by and introduced themselves. Everyone was so friendly and nice. No one gave her a hard time for just sitting there in the sweats, and no one looked at them judgmentally. In fact, everyone seemed really impressed that Jessie and Nika had taken time out of their day to spend time with the men in the gym. Some had even made comments to Jason and Cal that they would kill to have a girl who did that.

Nika decided then and there that this was something she would support Jason in. She would show up. She would cheer him on. She would be his companion and spend that time with him. It was clear that this was something important to them.

She came out of her reverie to see Jessie staring at her. "You're thinking it too, aren't you?"

"Thinking what?"

"Oh, I don't know. I'm thinking about how this might become more than just a once-in-a-while thing; it's an actual part of our routine.

Should we ask the boys what we should do if we wanted to work out with them?"

"Oh, I… uhhh…I hadn't gotten THAT far. But yeah, I was thinking about how I would find the time to come with Jason regularly. Everyone here is so nice."

"Do you really want to just sit here the whole time and just watch him?"

"Well, like I said, I hadn't gotten that far. But you are right. Sooner or later, my restless leg will get to me, and I'll start wondering what I could DO while I'm supporting him. I suppose we could ask them for a light workout, something that keeps the four of us, or at least the couples, in the same space. I don't want to come here and then just, you know, go to our separate places and then get back together when we're done." She remembered working out at the University with her then-boyfriend, and that was how it was. He would park her on the treadmill, and he would play basketball with his buddies on the courts.

Jessie scrunched her face up, "Oh yeah, like Travis."

"Travis, who?" Nika asked.

"Some guy I dated in high school, you've heard me mention him, he married my cousin, well he played football and I was in cheer, so we would work out together, but he was always in the weight room, and I was on the machines. We would meet after and be like, "Great workout together," but I always felt lonely."

"Yes! Like that! You always get me. OK, so let's talk to the boys tonight and set something up, but if they can't figure out how to keep us all together, then I'm out."

"It's a deal, me too."

They spent the rest of the afternoon watching the men, Cal, Jessie, and Jason, taking time out to explain certain things, such as timing, technique, and even the different colors of the weights, so she could understand how to calculate the bar. After showering and cleaning up,

Jason and Nika said bye to Cal and Jessie, who had plans to continue their date throughout the weekend.

As they walked out to Jason's truck, Jason shook his head. "I still can't get over Cal. I've never seen him like this. It's great, Jessie's great." Grabbing Nika's hand, he pulled her in close. "I'm so glad I met you."

"I'm glad I met you, too."

He leaned down to kiss her. "You're cold. Get in the truck."

As he stowed his gear in the back seat and climbed into the driver's side, he asked, "So, did you have a good time?"

"I did! Everyone was so nice and welcoming, and it was nice that Jessie was there. We got to talk and connect. This is something we haven't had a lot of time to do since I started seeing you, and now, clearly, there will be less time with her and Cal. Did you have a good time?"

"Oh, babe, it was so good to have you there. I did great on my lifts, and my girl was there. I couldn't have asked for better, to be honest."

Nika blushed. "Soooo Jessie and I were talking."

"Why do I have this overwhelming urge to say 'oh oh'?"

Nika laughed. "We're not THAT much trouble. Anyways, we were talking, and we were thinking that going to the gym with you two would be something we would like to do, like every time that you go, I'd like to come."

"Seriously, babe? I am not here to change you."

He tried valiantly to keep the excitement out of his voice.

"No, Jessie and I were talking about it, and I had a moment where I realized that I just like being with you and supporting you. This was important enough to you that you asked me to come, and once there, I really saw how much this meant to you, not only the working out but having me there. I couldn't help but overhear more than a few of the guys and girls saying that they wished their partners would join them in the gym, and I realized that this desire is what prompted you to ask, and I want to be a part of it. As I said earlier, people are friendly, and everyone is supportive. You and Cal crack jokes, and it's just easy being there with you."

He leaned in and took her hand. Keeping his eyes on the road. "Are you sure?"

She nodded and then added, "We do have some conditions, though."

"We?"

"Jessie and I, she's having this same conversation with Cal."

"Oh. I see, and your conditions?"

"We want something that is either us four together working out or you and me working out."

He frowned.

"Ugh, I'm not explaining this well. When I was at University, I dated a guy who worked out with me. Or rather, we would "go workout," she quoted in air quotes, "but what that meant was we went to the University gym together, and he would drop me off on the machines and go off and do his thing, then when we were done, we could get changed and leave together. All we did together was come and go; everything else was… lonely, and I, frankly, felt inadequate."

"Oh, babe, not even a little bit. You are perfect. But are you saying you want to lift weights with us?" His voice held a tiny tremble of excitement.

"Does that turn you on?"

"Absofuckinglutely, babe."

"I'm not sure if I will like it or even be good at it. I'm not sure if it's for me, but I don't want to be there if I don't get to be there with you. I want to share the same space and spend time with you, cracking jokes with you and doing things with you."

He tried to keep his voice casual. "I can build you a program, a workout program that will keep you very close to me and will let you work out. Something where we can use the same space in different ways. I can do that very easily."

"Then I want to come with you."

I go four to five days a week, babe. "

"Then I'd better pick up some more leggings and sweats, then!" She said jauntily.

He parked the truck in front of her house and grabbed her face, pulling her in close for a scorching kiss. "I think I love you."

"Did you mean to say that?"

"Not this early, but I'm just so dazzled by you I can't think of anything else to say, but that's all I'm feeling right now."

"I think I must love you if I'm contemplating doing these things with you, too." She laughed. "My mom is going to lose her damn mind when she hears I'm in the gym. She's been pushing me to go for ages."

"Oh?"

Nika got quiet. "My mom was a residential school survivor. For the first 5-10 years of my life, she drank a lot. Finding peace in the gym saved her. You always want to share the things that give you any semblance of peace and grounding. For her, it's her classes." Nika laughed with a lump in her throat. "Gotta go to my classes, honey! I'll be home after my classes are done. In a way, you can say she replaced one addiction with another, but at least she was there, present, and available to be a good mother to me and my sister when she found the gym. But yeah, she's going to think I lost my goddamn mind, but she'll be happy, and I'm warning you now, she will insist on meeting you." Nika wiped some tears from her eyes.

"Oh, honey, I didn't know."

"I know, I don't like to talk about it, but it wasn't horrible. I was very young, and my aunties took me in. I just thought all the kids spent every other week with a different auntie or their Kokum. Kokum means grandmother. It got harder to hide from me once I started school, but even then, I just passed it off as if we were a close family. I think I was about 8 when I realized that this wasn't just being a close family but that my mom was sick and needed help, more help than we as a family could give her. I got really, really, really mad at her and said some typically 8-year-old mean things, and she decided then and there she was going to dry out so she could spank me properly." Nika laughed. "She went away for a few months. After she dried out, she came back for me, hugged and thanked me, and we cried. Funny how things turn out."

"I'm sorry, baby."

"It's OK, I'm OK. It's just one of those tough conversations to have with people. Like, how are they going to react? How will their reaction make me feel? I've felt so bad and ashamed of things like this in my past for so long. I don't ever want to open myself up to let someone make me feel that again."

"I understand." He bundled her up and pulled her into his lap, the steering wheel digging slightly into her hip. He pulled her in for a deep, long kiss. As he pulled away, he said, "I don't ever want to make you feel any of those things." He kissed her forehead and hugged her close to his chest. They sat like that for a while, and then he pulled away and said, "Let's go inside and watch a movie or a show and cuddle."

"I would like that very much."

He got out of the truck and grabbed their gear while she got out. They were making their way up the drive to the door when she put her hand on his arm, stopping him. "Jason, I just want to say this before I get too scared to say it. But thank you for listening, and I think I love you too."

He dropped everything on the grass and pulled her up into his arms, kissing her fiercely as if he couldn't get enough of her. His mouth devoured her as she grabbed his shoulders and pulled him in close, hugging his heat close to her body. He dropped their gym bags on the ground and cupped her ass, holding her against his rock-hard groin. Breaking off the kiss to pull back for a second, he muttered.

"Ah, baby, let's get your hot little body into the house and on that couch. I don't think I can make it up the stairs this time."

She nodded and held on tight.

He groaned softly into her chest while he fumbled for the door and dumped her on the couch, following her down, grinding her into the couch.

"I can't even tell you how much this is heaven," as he leaned in for a deep kiss.

Hours later, he groaned and lifted his head up from her chest. "Sorry, I fell asleep after that, but I was toast."

Her left arm was asleep, and her legs were a bit chilly, but she actually didn't mind just lying on the couch half-naked, post-coital, while he napped on her. She swept his bangs out of his eyes and said, "I didn't mind. You were warm, and I felt good, too." He chuckled. "I should run out and grab the gym bags. They are still on the front lawn."

"While you do that, I'm going to run up and start the shower."

"Sounds good, babe."

Stretching luxuriously under the hot spray, she smiled as she thought of just how perfectly right her life had been lately. Hearing the door open and Jason start to strip down, she warns him, "Be careful. It's hot."

He grunted and came under the hot spray, wrapping his arms around her. His face was serious and moody.

"What's wrong?"

"I don't know how to tell you this."

She braced, knowing that what was going to come out of his mouth wasn't going to be good news.

"But?" she asked.

"Well, I went out to get our gym bags, and yours had the word WHORE written on it in Sharpie, and mine was torn apart and completely destroyed."

She gasped. "Who would do this?"

"Hon, do you have an ex-boyfriend or someone in your past who's reached out recently?"

"No. I never really dated much before you. Most of my exes are married with kids. Happily married at that."

"Do you know anyone who might be angry at you for dating? Cause, honey, first the roses and now this, I think you have a stalker."

"No! I can't think of anyone who would be like that. That's crazy!" He hugged her close. "It's OK, we'll figure this out, but these are all adding up to someone who is deeply disturbed and clearly getting angry."

"What should I do?"

"We're going to keep our eyes out. We'll call the police and file a report. I don't think there's much they can do, but we'll at least start making the authorities aware that there's an issue. I just set the alarm up, and I put the code on a piece of paper in your kitchen. We'll be more diligent about making sure it's on when you are out and when we are home."

She nodded.

"And babe," he paused, staring into her eyes. "I think maybe I should start staying here all the time. Like not move in, but you know, move in." he waited for her response.

She trembled and asked softly, "Would you be OK with that?"

"I want you safe, and I want to be around in case you ever don't feel safe. I don't like this. At all. That is fueling an intense need in me to be close to you. My apartment is too small, it's not ideal, it's also not close to either of our jobs, whereas your house is actually really close to both our jobs, it's close to our gym, and I just think it makes more sense."

"I'm going to go to my place and grab some stuff that I need, plus the extra gym stuff I need that got destroyed. I want you to come with me. I'm going to keep my apartment, though. I can go back anytime if this isn't working out. OK?"

"I would feel a lot better if you were here with me. I'm very overwhelmed by the idea of you moving in, but I can handle you staying here indefinitely."

"I gotta look after my girl. We'll try this for two weeks, and if it's working out, I'll maybe direct my mail here so I don't have to head back to the apartment every couple of days to get it. OK?"

"You've given this a lot of thought."

"Nah, my heart just about went into my throat when I saw my gym stuff strewn over your lawn. As I was cleaning it up, everything just came together. I don't like this, not one bit, so the logical part of me didn't take too long to figure out I have to be here all the time."

"I really appreciate you doing this for me. I know it's not ideal. I mean, we just started dating!"

He gripped her chin and pulled her face up to look at him. "I wasn't joking earlier when I said I think I love you. I would do just about anything to keep you safe, and none of this is hard or difficult. What do you think of a dog?"

"A dog?"

"I just think it adds an extra layer of security."

"Jason, if we adopt a dog, what happens if it doesn't work out? Dog custody arrangements?"

"Well, I mean, it's been done. I read an article about a couple doing that."

She laughed. "OK then, do we have time for a dog?"

"Sure, we'll make time."

"Do you like dogs?"

"Me?" He asked. "Yeah, I like dogs. We always had dogs growing up. In fact, my parents still have Sully, the dog we adopted the year before I moved out of the home. Wait, do you like dogs?"

"My one aunt always had a dog. I loved her dog. Yeah, I like dogs. They always seemed like a big responsibility. I'm shy about big responsibilities. I can't even tell you how much I agonized over pulling the trigger on buying this house. Knowing I was committing to something so big!"

"OK then, this weekend, we'll look around for a dog. Something larger that will intimidate people and stop them from harassing you."

"I don't want one of those super aggressive dogs that attack anything that moves towards me."

"No, no, we want a big baby of a sweetheart, just something that looks super intimidating. The knowledge that there's a pet in the house is usually a deterrent for most people anyway. But this guy, this person, they know where you live and are a little more determined than your common break-and-enter thief. This person may be deterred by the addition of a pet. They may not, which is why I'm still coming to stay with you." He said with a stubborn set to his chin.

"Jason," she put her hand on his arm. "I'm glad you are coming to stay here for a bit. I can't think of anything that makes me feel safer."

He looked down at her hand on his arm and said, "You remember the last time you put your hand on me like that and said 'Jason'? It ended with me taking a nap."

She laughed. "Alright, alright," as she pulled back.

"Hey, I didn't say you should move." He embraced her in a big bear hug and moved them both under the hot spray.

"Let's get washed up, grab some stuff at my place, and then maybe look online at dogs to check out tomorrow."

"Sounds like a plan."

She couldn't help but feel safe and happy with Jason. No matter what was going on, she knew he was in her corner, and that was more than enough.

They took his truck to his apartment. It was a pleasant place, much smaller than her place, but as he stated, he didn't need much. He did mention that it was close to his parents' place, and she understood his need to be close to them in case they needed anything. He spoke of them with love, and she could hear his need to protect them in his voice, much like his need to protect her. She couldn't help but admire how devoted he was to the people he cared about, and it filled her with warmth and love to know he wanted to provide her with that sense of security.

They managed to get everything he would need into one load. He emptied out his fridge and freezer, too, so that she would have lots of options for meals over the next few weeks, and he wouldn't have to come back anytime soon. As they drove away, he mentioned coming back next weekend just to check on the place and get his mail. Again, she stated that she would go with him.

"Are we going to go everywhere together? All the time?"

"Why? Is that a problem?" He frowned.

"NO! No, I just don't know if I'm overreacting or not. Am I overreacting by feeling this scared?"

"Well, babe," Jason glanced at her as he grabbed her hand. "I don't want you scared. That's part of why I'm planning to be with you, but some guy, some person out there, took the time to write a really disgusting word on your gym bag and literally tore mine to shreds. They know where you live, and they seem to be pretty brave doing an action like that in broad daylight, on your lawn, while we are at home. Someone is either crazy or extremely upset, and I don't think that's something you are overreacting to."

Nika shivered. "I don't know who would even care that much. I have been racking my brain, and I can't even think of a single person who would be that mad at me."

"It's OK, babe, we'll figure it out." He pulled her hand up to his lips and kissed the top.

Nika looked out the window at the passing scenery. "I should probably call my family and let them know of the changes. I wouldn't want them to stop by and be surprised. I don't really want to tell them. It's embarrassing."

"Honey, you did nothing wrong."

"It feels like I did."

"You did nothing wrong." He squeezed her hand. "When we get home, we'll unload the truck and call the cops. We'll make a statement, and then you can call your mom, and I'll call my parents and let them know I'll be staying at your place for a while. It'll all be OK."

"My mom isn't going to take it well; she'll probably call the aunties, hop in the car, and head over. You may meet a lot of very angry ladies this evening. Just a heads up."

Jason paled a bit. "How angry?"

"Oh, you know, mad as hell, but with cookies and comfort."

He laughed. "I think I can handle a couple of old ladies."

"You call them old, and I'm not responsible for what happens to you in my living room."

"Noted."

He parked the truck, and they hopped out. He put his arm around her shoulders, and they made their way up to the front porch, where they saw her plant that used to be on her front porch table smashed to the floor. Jason hugged her close as he looked around the neighborhood, but he couldn't see anything out of the ordinary. So they trudged inside as he promised to clean it up once the cops had been by.

She set the alarm and went to make coffee while Jason called the cops to file a report. When he was done, he came up behind her and wrapped his arms around her. Turning her around to look at him, he said, "They will be here in about half an hour."

She shook her head in acknowledgment and grabbed her coffee while handing him his. Then, she made her way to the living room couch to wait.

She curled up on the couch, and he sat down beside her and pulled her into his lap.

The next hour was grueling and uncomfortable. Jessie texted just as the cops arrived, and Nika filled her in while Jason filled the authorities in and showed them the various damages.

"Do you need me to come over for support?"

"No, I think Jason and I have this handled. He wants us to pick up a dog, too. Something imposing on the outside but a teddy bear on the inside."

"You mean like him?" Nika laughed. Jessie continued on. "I'm really glad he's taking this seriously and making arrangements for you to be safe. When we left the gym, Cal asked if I had an alarm system at my place, and when I admitted no, he got upset and promised to do the same thing Jason did for you. I have to admit, while I like being an independent woman, this protecting stuff is outta sight. I feel all warm and fuzzy when I think of it."

Nika laughed again. "Yeah, they do alright, don't they?"

Jessie texted back. "Do you think you should mention that guy who sent you the weird note through the speed-dating organization?"

"What, that guy? I mean, he was rude, but I don't know. Is being rude wrong?"

"Noooo, but you guys had a pretty heated exchange AT the speed dating event, and then he sent you that weird note through them that just screams incel to me. I got the heebie-jeebies as well as righteously mad when you told me about it."

"Yeah, he was super weird in that note. Especially after how much we did not hit it off at the event. OK, I mean, it's likely nothing, but I will mention it."

She looked up to see Jason staring at her questioningly and the cops curiously. "I gotta go, Jessie. People are looking at me."

"Bye, sistah! Talk to you tomorrow at work! I'm going to tell Cal about this if you don't mind."

"Sure, I'm over the shock and embarrassment now. You can tell Cal all about it. Bye."

She put her phone down and cleared her throat. "So Jessie reminded me about this one thing."

"Oh?" asked Jason.

"So Jason and I met at a speed dating event that I went to with my best friend Jessie, whom I just finished talking with."

The cops nodded. She went on to explain the events and then started telling them about the note he sent through the organizers.

"He said what?!" Jason exploded.

Nika looked up at him in shock. "Well, he said…."

"I heard what you said, babe," gripping her shoulders and turning to look at him. "You are perfect. Absolutely perfect. No one should ever say that to you, EVER."

The one cop cleared his throat and interrupted. "I'm going to need to see that email, Ma'am."

Nika looked for her phone. "Oh sure, yeah. I think I still have it."

She scrolled through her emails while the cops took the time to explain to Jason that not much could be done, that she and Jason had to be hyper-aware of their surroundings, be careful, lock up properly, keep to themselves, and not increase their social bubble to include people they don't know and trust. No big gatherings, etc.

She handed the cop her phone, and he read the email. "OK, can you forward that to me?" He handed her her phone back and went over his email with her. She sent it to him, and they thanked them for the information. They would make a report but remind them again that there wasn't much they could do or go on and that they should keep alert.

As Jason closed the door, he turned around and said to her, "I'm going to want to see that email."

"Are you sure?"

"Absofucking-lutely."

"You're mad."

"No, babe, I'm furious."

"At me for not telling you? I didn't even remember until Jessie reminded me."

"No honey, never at you, at this schmuck that thinks it's OK to say and do these things to women. What he did and said to you is never OK. And if it turns out this is the guy that's trying to scare you, then that's really not OK."

"Jessie said he sounded like an incel kind of guy."

"That's exactly what he sounds like. He sounds like a guy who can't get a date because he's not a very good person at all, and instead of trying to change who he is, he's going to blame you, a woman, for it. That's the very definition of incel."

"So what do we do now?"

"We tell the family, and we hunker down to go to bed. It's been a very, very long day." Jason looped an arm around her shoulder and pulled her in for a hug as he kissed her forehead. "Then tomorrow we go and look for puppies," he grinned excitedly.

"Oh boy. Lotsa changes this weekend."

"Yup, but anything for my girl."

Nika texted her mom, who immediately set up a group chat between the whole family. Nika laughed ruefully. There was just no getting around the fact that all her aunts and uncles would be involved. At least her Kokum didn't have a phone.

Auntie Grace texted, "What happened, Nika?"

Nika explained everything.

Auntie Teresa interrupted, "They did what?"

Nika's Mom, Holly, texted, "We're coming over."

Nika texted back, "Mom, it's late. I have had a very big day. Can you come over tomorrow?"

"I'll be there bright and early."

Auntie Grace responded, "Me too!"

Then Auntie Teresa.

"Me three! Uncle Mike will be with me. He wants to get a measure of this, Jason, and the security system he set up."

"Nika, darling, we'll all be there. This is your kokum texting, and I'm bringing the bannock," suddenly popped up from Auntie Grace's texts. Of course, Auntie Grace would be at Kokums this weekend.

"Yes, Kokum."

"Grace will bring the casserole, and Teresa will make the bison stew. Holly, you roast the root vegetables."

Suddenly, two other "Yes, Mom" popped into the chat.

Nika texted, "Jason wants us to go shopping for a dog, something intimidating looking but a sweetheart inside. So we also need to do that tomorrow."

"No, no, no. Your Auntie Teresa and Uncle Mike's oldest son, Gabe's dog, just had a passel of pups. They will bring one for you. Right, Teresa?"

"Yes, Mom. I'll tell Mike and Gabe to pick out a good one from the litter. We'll bring all the supplies you need, too, honey."

"Thanks, Aunties."

Nika was filled with a strong warmth of gratitude for her family. They weren't perfect, but the love was amazing.

She put down her phone and went to the kitchen to pour herself a glass of wine while waiting for Jason to be done with his call.

He sauntered in 10 minutes later and grabbed a beer from the fridge.

"So?" he asked.

She sighed. "Well, we have a dog, and I managed to convince them to come tomorrow instead."

"We have a dog?"

"Yeah, Auntie Teresa and Uncle Mike's oldest son, Gabe, his dog just had some pups, and he and Uncle Mike are going to pick the best one for the job and bring it tomorrow." She grinned and rolled her eyes. "Along with bannock, bison stew, casserole, and roasted veggies."

"What are they feeding an army?"

"This is what my family does. People are in pain, or sad, or hurt, and they bring out the food and comfort."

"I think it's great."

"Fair warning: Uncle Mike specifically said he wants to check you out and the system you installed. Just so you know."

"Oh, Jeez, the pressure. OK. It'll be OK."

"How did your call go?"

"Well, my parents want to meet you right away, which I told them to back off, and I would introduce you to them when I felt it was a good time. My mom can be super pushy, but I got it handled. My dad is the quiet type, kind of sits in the background, and lets Mom call the shots. He didn't say much. However, he did mention that he had run into Cal at the hardware store the other day, and Cal had mentioned that I had a new girl. So he already knew. Mom was not pleased about that, and I hung up on her, giving him the shakedown on how they need to communicate better." Jason snorted. "I don't know how she expects him to get a word in edgewise."

He grabbed her hand and pulled her towards the stairs, "Let's go to bed. Today was a long day, and it looks like tomorrow will be even longer."

She let him drag her up the stairs. As they readied for bed, she said, "Jason, thanks for being here. This seems so much easier to handle with you around."

"Anytime, babe, I'm here for you." They crawled under the covers, and she sidled up to him, laying her head in the curve of his arm. She yawned once and then fell asleep.

Chapter 16

Nika was up bright and early, getting the house ready for the influx of family that would be showing up. Knowing her Kokum and her mom, they would be here much earlier than a normal person would appear. Sure enough, at 8 am, she heard her aunt's minivan driving up to the front of her porch. She yelled up to Jason, who was still getting dressed upstairs, that people were arriving and went to the front door to let people in. She disengaged the alarm system and opened the door, watching her aunt, Mom, and Kokum walking up the pathway to the front door.

"Hi Mom, Hi Kokum, Hi Auntie Grace."

Holly kissed her daughter on the cheek. "Auntie Teresa, Uncle Mike, and Gabe will be here later with the pup. They had to stop and get some supplies."

"They didn't have to do that. Jason and I could have done that."

"They know they don't have to, but they love you, and they will do that for you." Holly frowned.

"I know Mama."

Kokum reached up to kiss Nika on the cheek. "Taanshi, my Cinnamon Sugar, are you OK? You look radiant, but there are ghosts around your eyes."

Nika sighed, and Kokum always looked at the center of her. "I'm fine, Kokum. I feel scared, and I don't like feeling like someone else is interfering in how I live my life, but I'm being careful, and I'm in a good place with a good man."

"You love him."

"How do you know?"

"You glow when you talk about him. There's a smile in your eyes."

"You just might be right."

Auntie Grace kissed her cheek. "Ma is right, you know. You have a softness, almost fragility about you, as if we talked too loud, you might break, but there's also happiness there."

"Come in, Auntie. I have missed you all."

"We have always missed our girl, living in the big city, making those beaucoup bucks."

Nika laughed. "Oh, if only."

She heard Jason clumping down the stairs, then felt the gasp from her mom. Her mom looked at her and signed, "Oh my. Hot."

Nika laughed again and nodded yes.

"You know sign language?" Jason asked, stunned.

"Yes! I guess it's never come up. I don't really speak it well. I'm a better reader, mostly because I don't need it to communicate. I just need it to hear. My family is very adept at it, however, as they have often needed it to communicate with me. Anyways, where are my manners? This is my Auntie Grace, my mom Holly, and my Kokum Patience."

"Beautiful names for beautiful ladies."

"Oh, I'm going to like this man," said Patience as she walked up to him, gave him a hug, and then turned her face and lifted her cheek. Jason looked at Nika's askance. She giggled.

"You're supposed to kiss it. It's quite the honor."

"Ah," he said as he bent down to the little woman and kissed her softly on the cheek. She patted the top of his head. "There's a good boy, so you are the one that's going to look after my Cinnamon Sugar."

"Oh, Kokum!" Nika protested while blushing.

Jason replied. "Sure am."

Nika's Kokum looped an arm in his, and while he led her to the kitchen, she asked him, "Do you know why I call her Cinnamon Sugar?"

Nika put her head in her hands. "Someone save me." Holly hugged her from behind, then signed, "You know she loves you and is incredibly worried about you."

Nika shook her head. "I know."

She walked into the kitchen to catch her Kokum, saying, "So look at me and my Holly, we're brown-eyed, black-haired tiny people, and when Holly was pregnant, we were all sure she would have this tiny brown-eyed, black-haired doll. We knew it was a girl, so I started calling her Cinnamon sugar, but boy, were we all surprised at this blonde baby with bright eyes that joined our lives, and the name stuck." Kokum laughed that big, deep-belly laugh that she had. Jason joined in with her while looking up at Nika with a big smile on his face. He replied to her, Kokum, "That sounds about right. Nika doesn't seem like the type to ever do what you would expect."

"Speaking of which," Holly said, "What's this I hear about the gym?"

"Oh yes, Jason goes to the gym regularly, and he asked me to come with him. I did this Saturday. In fact, Jessie and I both went since Jessie's boyfriend, Cal, works out with Jason."

"Does she have a boyfriend? Who's also a friend of Jason's?"

Nika laughed. "Yes, Jessie did, too. She was a cheerleader in high school, remember? So she's always been active, unlike me. She met Cal the night Cal came over to help Jason install the security system, and they hit it off faster than anything I've ever seen."

"Oh, that makes sense," interjected Auntie Grace. "That's good for Jessie. She's a good person. I've always liked her. She's kind and respectful. A good girl."

Nika laughed. "What about all those times when you insisted I wouldn't have gotten into half the trouble I did if it wasn't for Jessie!"

Grace got a little twinkle in her eye as she fired back. "Oh, I know you're the one with the big ideas. Jessie just always knew how to make them work. While she's a good girl, the two of you together are pure trouble."

Nika mumbled under her breath, "We aren't that bad."

"Awww, honey." Grace fired back. "Everyone grows up sometimes."

Everyone laughed, and suddenly, the doorbell went. Holly stood up from the table. "Grace and Ma, you keep unpacking the food. I'll get it. Nika, visit with your family and help Jason fit in."

Nika looked at Jason, and he grinned at her. "I see where the drill sergeant comes from."

Holly grinned back at him. "Damn straight, we raise strong women here."

Grace and Patience just nodded their heads in agreement while Nika blushed. Jason shot back. "Just the way I like them!"

As Holly left the kitchen, Jason said, "So, are we going to talk about how you know sign language?"

Patience looked surprised. "You know she can't hear, right?"

Jason nodded, "But she never even hinted that she did anything other than read lips".

Grace interrupted, "Oh, that's because she doesn't like talking about it. She likes to pretend it doesn't exist and muddle through. Always making things harder than they need to be."

Nika protested. "Not everyone knows the sign, and it's safer to assume they don't."

"But I'll learn." Jason quietly said.

Patience patted him on the hand. "Of course, you will, my boy, because you love her. I see it."

Jason looked at her. "I do? You can see that?"

She shook her head sagely. "You may not know it yet; your head gets in front of your heart, but I do, I know, and I see." Grace was nodding her head. "She really does see. Trust her."

Jason squared his shoulders. "Well then," as he stared intensely at Nika, "I guess I do."

She blushed furiously.

Patience said, "First, there's the alphabet. Once you know that, you can fingerspell everything until you learn all the words." As she walked Jason through the alphabet, Holly walked in with Auntie Teresa, Uncle Mike, and Gabe. Jessie followed up behind, talking on the phone. Gabe was holding a small kennel. Uncle Mike was holding some big bags full of things.

In his booming voice, Uncle Mike said, "Dog's here!" while walking up to Nika to kiss her on the cheek. She hugged him back. "Thanks, Uncle Mike and Gabe."

"Anytime, Sugar."

Auntie Teresa came up behind Uncle Mike and darted in for a hug. "I'm so glad you are taking this seriously and being ultra-careful. Now, where's this man I've heard about?" She turns about and opens up her arms. "You must be Jason. Come here for a hug, honey."

Jason gets up from the table and leans in for a hug. "You guys sure like your hugs."

"Better get used to it, man," Gabe retorted. "They'll hug you all day long." He held out a hand, and they shook.

Uncle Mike looked Jason up and down, and then he said, "So you want to show me that alarm system you put in to look after our girl?"

Teresa quipped, "Give the boy a break, Mike. You just got here. They need to meet the puppy, which likely needs to sniff the backyard, and you don't need to be giving Nika's man a hard time."

"I don't mind. I'll show him the system right now while you all calm down the puppy. I'm sure there are too many voices in here anyway."

Gabe looked frantically between the group of ladies and his dad. It was clear he did not want to be stuck in the kitchen with his aunties and mom, but he had a responsibility to introduce the dog. Nika took pity on him. "Hey Gabe, wanna go into the living room with me, and we'll release the puppy so he can sniff around? Or do you think he needs to pee?"

Gabe looked relieved. He probably didn't want to get the third degree about his university progress, like at the last family get-together. Auntie Teresa was determined that it was taking him too long to finish up. "Yeah, cousin. Let's do that," he signed.

They left the aunts behind in the kitchen to finish preparing the mountain of food they had brought, while she and Gabe headed to the living room to let the puppy out. She could see Jason and Uncle Mike deep in conversation by the security system, and they both looked really involved in the conversation. She saw Uncle Mike laugh and knew they were OK. Jessie trailed behind the two of them, opting to come into the living room. She sat on the couch and waved to get Nika's attention.

"Hey, I invited Cal to come over. I know that it's a lot of people, but when I met Teresa, Mike, and Gabe on your front step and heard Mike saying he was going to go over that system with a fine toothed comb, I knew that Cal coming over to help explain things, if needed, would be a good idea. Plus," she grinned, "I just want to see him."

Nika laughed. "It's OK, Jessie, the more the merrier, judging by the food everyone brought, and you are family as far as everyone is concerned, so you might as well let them meet your boyfriend too."

Gabe looked up from the kennel that he had placed on the floor, "Yeah, cuz, you might as well give them something else to talk about other than my education." He rolled his eyes.

Jessie laughed. "Oh, so now I'm your cousin too?"

"Anyone who distracts Ma from my classes is family to me." Gabe retorted.

"How much longer do you have anyway?" Nika asked.

"Oh, two years, but here's the thing, you don't really get anywhere with just a Psychology degree, so I dived right back in to get my Master's. I actually convocated this June, but since I wasn't "done school," Ma figured it wasn't worth really celebrating. You know her. She wants this whole thing done. She wants me to have a big snazzy career and bring in the "beaucoup bucks," and until then nothing else counts."

"You convocated? And didn't tell me?" Nika smacked his shoulder. "Well, Congratulations, Cousin!"

"Yeah, Congratulations!" quipped Jessie. "Your Masters degree, when it's done, is going to make us all look like slackers. Way to go, overachiever."

Nika laughed. "Oh god, I didn't think about that. Maybe we need to go back to school."

Jessie shook her head emphatically. "NOPE, that's a big Nope from me. I don't wanna."

Gabe knelt down by the kennel. Nika and Jessie followed suit.

"OK, so he doesn't have a name yet. I figured that I would leave that for you. He's the biggest of the litter and looks like a real badass. Has had his shots and is ready to be away from his Mama." He opened the kennel and reached in to bring out this black pit bull puppy with a white upside-down triangle on his chest. His big brown eyes looked frantically at everything while his tail hesitantly waved. Nika held out her hand palm down for him to sniff. He leaned in and sniffed, then licked it. She giggled.

Gabe gave the puppy to her to hold, and as she snuggled him in close, her cousin continued to sign. "I won't dock his tail or ears, which makes them look really serious and aggressive. I don't believe in it, so his ears will be a tad floppy, but with a face like that, he's still going to deter most people from thinking about breaking in. He'll grow into that mug, I promise. He'll be about 50-80 pounds and pure muscle. He needs to be spayed, and I trust that you will be responsible for doing that. Right?"

Nika nodded her head. "Absolutely. I'm glad you don't dock the tail or the ears; he's perfect." She cuddled him tight to her chest, and he sniffed and licked her hands and face.

"OH my god, Gabe, he's adorable. Does he have a sister or brother I could have?" Jessie squealed.

Gabe frowned, "Don't you live in an apartment condo? Do they allow pets?"

Jessie scratched behind the pup's ears. "I'd buy a house just to have something this cute."

Nika and Gabe laughed.

"Oh, Jessie, you are crazy."

Gabe muttered. "If you can have a pet, then yes, I'll let you have one of my pups. But only because you are family and single and a girl."

"I'm not single."

"Wait, you're dating too!?" Gabe looked crushed.

"What? You wanted to date me?" Jessie looked at him, shocked.

"Noooooooo." Gabe frowned, "I just don't need y'all married, dating, and working because I'll NEVER hear the end of it.", imitating his mom's voice, "Gabe, sweetie. I know you are still in school, but it's been SO LONG, and I want babies. Look at Nika and Jessie. They are going to give Holly babies soon! Are they even dating? Why can't my handsome young man give me babies?"

Nika and Jessie howled with laughter. "That's a LONG LONG LONG LONG way off." Nika snickered. "We just got a puppy for crying out loud. Hold your horses!"

Jason and Uncle Mike looked up to see what they were laughing about, and Jason's eyes lit up at the puppy in Nika's lap. He called over. "That's one gorgeous pup! Male?"

Gabe turned around to look at his dad and Jason, "Yup, biggest one of the litter. Nika has yet to name him."

Uncle Mike turned to Jason and said, "Gabe has the mom and dad, but neither is fixed. He doesn't breed them but just lets nature take its course. Sometimes, the dad gets a little too happy, and if anything, Gabe will prevent him from bothering the mom so as to rest her up a bit more. He takes this very seriously and humanely while making a pile of money for his top-shelf puppies, but still, my wife feels he's not successful." Mike shook his head ruefully.

Gabe grinned. "Gotta make those 'beaucoup bucks,' Dad," Nika and Jessie laughed and shook their heads. "Yup, that's how it works!"

"Well, son, I'm proud of what you do, no matter what your mama says, and she's proud too. She just wants to push you to be your best." Both Gabe and Uncle Mike cleared their throats awkwardly. "Thanks, Dad."

"Don't mention it, son. Seriously, we won't speak of this again." Mike grinned.

The doorbell rang, and Jason went to get it. Jessie called out as he was walking away, "That's probably Cal!"

Not even five minutes later, Jason came back to the living room with Cal. He made the introductions as Jessie got up from the floor to walk over to Cal to kiss him.

"So you two are dating too?" Uncle Mike asked. Jessie shook her head in affirmation. "So I gotta vet two men now?"

Cal looked taken aback. "Vet?"

Uncle Mike looked at him. "Yeah, when you date family, someone's gotta look out for them, so I'm going to have some questions for you, son. Let's go look at that system you two put in."

Jessie stood on tiptoe to kiss Uncle Mike's cheek. "Thanks, Uncle Mike."

"Anytime, Princess." he blushed.

Cal just looked confused. "You're related?"

Jessie shook her head no.

Mike grinned. "The minute Nika brought this little gal home, she became a part of the family, but blood or no blood, make no mistake, we look out for her."

Cal nodded his head. "All right then."

Jessie sat back down on the floor next to Nika. "He's so laid back and accepting. I just love it."

Gabe stood up. "Well, I'm going to leave you two alone to acclimate the pup. Maybe take him out to the backyard at some point and get him used to where he's going to do his business."

Nika nodded her head and looked up at Gabe. "Thank you. I know it came at a personal cost. I really appreciate it."

"Anytime, cousin, and I mean it. Anytime. Jessie, you figure out your apartment situation and let me know if I'm giving you one of this big boy's siblings."

Gabe pats the dog on the neck.

From the hallway, they heard Cal shout. "A dog, too?"

Everyone laughed. Gabe leaned down. "Don't worry, I'll explain." And he sauntered off to join the men in the hallway.

Nika snuggled the pup close. "I have no idea what to name him."

Jessie rubbed the top of his head. "I'm sure you and Jason will come up with a great name. Shall we take him into the kitchen to meet the ladies and then make our way to the backyard?"

"Yes, let's do that."

They got up and made their way into the kitchen. The pup enjoyed many tummy rubs and snuggles while they visited, and then they took him outside to let him sniff around. Auntie Teresa found the doggy bags in the supplies they brought for Nika and gave them to her. Nika and Jessie sat on the edge of the raised deck and chatted about how much their life had changed while they watched the pup explore his new home. Both of them marveled at how different things felt with these men in their lives.

Later that afternoon, everyone enjoyed a great big meal with lots of laughter and conversation as people passed around the pup for snuggles and enjoyed its antics as it learned its new home. It was a long but incredibly satisfying day. It was with gratefulness that Nika and Jason closed the door behind the last guest and took the time to just relax and chat while they readied the pup and themselves for bed.

Jason snuggled the pup in his chest. "Thought of any names yet?"

Nika shook her head. "That's eluding me. I thought maybe Thor, but he's too dark for that. I considered Loki then, but so far, he's not mischievous enough for that. Any ideas?"

"Do you want a mythological name?"

"I want a strong, confident name that he will grow into. Something with weight and impact."

"Strong. Got it. What about Mack, Pork Chop, or Tank?"

Nika burst out into giggles. "Well, Tank is about the closest of those three, but still not it. But Pork chop?"

"Hey, I'm just helping! What about something in Metis?"

Nika teared up a little at his suggestion. "Well, strong in Michif, our language, is Maashkowishiiw, and strongman is aen nom aen mashkowishiit, both of which are really long and difficult for most people to pronounce."

Jason stumbled over. "Maashkowishiiw. Yeah, I mean, I'll get it right with practice, but you're right. We could do Maash?"

Nika: "We could, but then it doesn't mean anything. It's just a nonsensical word, in essence. It definitely wouldn't mean strong anymore."

"OK then, back to the drawing board. What about King, Duke, Boss, or Remo?"

"Wait, hold up. Remo? I think we're getting there. But it's also close to Nemo. He is NOT a clownfish."

"LOL. Well, Captain Nemo was an intrepid explorer. What about Bear? Bruiser? Or Bourbon? Maybe Conall?"

"YES!" She jumped up. "Conall the Bear, or Bear for short."

Jason laughed, "Well, that's certainly a name to grow into! But done! I accept this name. He is now Conall the Bear. Or just Bear."

Nika snuggled him into her chest while he tried to lick her face. "Hey, Bear, welcome to the crew."

Chapter 17

Jason and Nika fell into a pretty easy routine for the week. She would wake up first and get ready for her day, and he would wake up later and see her off to the office. Bear would play with them in the morning, and then he would be kenneled until Jason came home for lunch. Then kenneled again until Nika came home from work. Jessie had filled Terrell in, so that Nika didn't have to, and he had instructed the front desk security at their office building to be extra sharp and aware of all newcomers and strangers.

Then, after a day of mind-numbing numbers, she would head home to prepare supper for the two of them, play with Bear, and walk him. Then, when Jason got home, they would hit the gym, often meeting Cal and Jessie there. The four of them became fast friends, with Cal and Jason both building routines that kept Jessie and Nika close to their area so they could keep an eye out. After working out, Nika and Jason would go home, make the supper she had prepped, play and cuddle with Bear, and, depending on how much energy they all had, take a quick walk to tire out the pup. Then, they would snuggle in to watch a show and head up to bed. The routine was comforting to her as well as exciting: so many changes, a new pup to take care of, and a warm man in her bed. She liked these new additions to her lifestyle. She felt purposeful and proactive, and it distracted her from the stress of worrying about who was out there who seemed to get their kicks out of terrorizing her.

On Thursday, she got a text message from Jason. "Babe, someone tried to break into the house. I came home to the front door, where the key lock was all scratched up, the alarm was blaring, and Bear was pretty upset. It looks like once the alarm started squealing, they took off. So that worked. I got a notification on my phone, so I left work early to see if it was a false alarm, and it wasn't."

"OHmigod! Why didn't I get a notification? I'll head right home now!"

"I've got it under control if you would rather stay at work. They didn't get in; they clearly were mad that they couldn't get in, and they kicked the pane of glass in the side panel of the door. It's cracked but not broken. I've called the cops, and they are sending someone out. Maybe Cal is right, and we should look at putting up a video camera, too."

"It's my home, and I'm coming home. I'll be there in about 40 minutes. We can talk about the camera then"

She jumped up from her desk and grabbed her things, shutting stuff down quickly while she texted Jessie and Terrell about what was happening. Terrell told her to go home and that he would handle the team. Jessie asked if she needed to come with her, and Nika declined.

She raced home, trying hard not to panic, and when she got there, the cops were already there.

As she walked into her home, she found Jason snuggling a now sleeping Bear while he explained to the cops what he found when he got home. The cops nodded at her, and when Jason finished explaining, the one looked at her and said, "I'm glad you are taking this seriously, letting him move in, and getting a dog. All good deterrents because I don't like this one bit. Your man talked to his friend who set up the alarm system, and they are going to put in cameras at the front entrance, too. Sooner or later, this guy will make a mistake, and we'll catch him, especially with all the precautions you've put into place. Don't take this to mean you can relax. Someone is very determined to get to you, and you need to keep up the hyperawareness. My partner," he pointed at the cop standing next to him, "walked over to your neighbor's, and they saw a skinny man in a ball cap walk up to your door and then leave in a hurry. They figured it was an Amazon delivery guy, but clearly, it was your intruder. They promised to keep an eye out for the guy and try to pay more attention to the details next time. She also mentioned that she was pretty sure that person was the same person who dropped off the flowers for you before.

She said she was certain they were wearing the same ball cap and jacket. So we'll add that to our case file report."

Nika nodded and hugged herself. "Thanks, officers. I really don't like this at all."

One officer put his hand on her arm. "Look, you've done everything right. It should be OK. We'll catch this guy." As they prepared to leave her house, the primary officer looked at Jason and said, "Put those cameras in sooner rather than later."

"Got it," Jason said.

As they closed the door on the police, she looked at Jason. "Why did the alarm system notify you and not me?"

Jason sighed. "Because with all the stuff going on, I only put it on my phone. I never set you up for it. I'm sorry. I know that bothered you."

"Yeah, it bothered me a lot. But I understand. It's been crazy these past weeks."

"Why don't you give me your phone? I'll upload it now, program it, and run it through with you. How does that sound?"

"Sure! I'm home for the day, so I'm going to make some popcorn and snuggle up with Bear."

"Yeah, I told my boss I wasn't going back to the shop today either, so I'll join you two, maybe put on a movie?"

"Sounds great."

"Cal is going to pick up some camera equipment after he's done work. We will meet at the gym, and then he and Jessie will come back home with us and install that."

"How much do I owe Cal for all this work?"

"Not a cent, honey. Cal and I figured it out. I'm going to do some quid pro quo and work on a few things for him."

"Are you sure?"

"Absofucking-lutely, babe."

"OK then." She snuggled into his chest with Bear curled up in her lap. She unlocked her phone and handed it over to Jason while she picked a movie for them to watch. Something fun and mindless with lots of explosions seemed to be the right ticket.

Cal came back to their place after the gym. Jessie, of course, tailed along with him. The men got the cameras installed in no time, and the four of them spent the rest of the evening having a drink and playing with Bear.

Chapter 18

The days passed in a blur of loving nights and a routine during the day that brought comfort while also keeping her busy so she didn't have too much time to think about who would want to mess with her.

After a couple of weeks, Jason and she were sitting on the couch watching a show when he said, "I think I would like you to meet my parents. Would that be OK?"

"Sure. When did you want to do that?"

"Well, my mom is hounding me, so perhaps sooner rather than later?"

"What did you have in mind? Do we go see them? Or they come here?"

"Well, I was thinking that we would go to their place. I didn't want to overstep and invite them here when I know things are feeling pretty violated as it stands."

"Jason, this is kinda your place too now."

"No, I know, but I'm still maintaining the illusion of having my own place, and so I've been super respectful in keeping this place as yours in my mind, with the idea that I'm visiting for a long time. I don't contribute to the bills or mortgage, and I'm pretty much freeloading here," he grinned ruefully. "I haven't done that since my early 20s."

Nika laughed. "Well, do you want them here?"

"I just think that they are going to want to meet the pup and see my new "digs," so to speak, that having them here would make more sense than going to their place in terms of showing them all the changes in my life. However, it's a lot to ask of you, having two new strangers come into your home."

"Jason, I don't mind. I think you're right. There's a lot to show them; your life has changed dramatically since we started dating, and it's easier to show them than just talk about it. I'm very much OK with the idea of them coming here to meet me."

"OK then, I'll let them know. I'll schedule it for next weekend, as we have that obedience school thing with Bear coming up all this weekend. Sounds good?"

"That's fine."

"Cal clearly knows your family. Should you invite Jessie and Cal as icebreakers? Or do you want it to just be us and your parents?"

"You know that's an idea. Let me think about it. I can definitely see the allure, and it would help make it feel a little less like a "Meet the Parents" kind of deal."

"You think about it. I'm good with whatever you decide."

He kissed the top of her forehead. "I am so glad you are in my life. You make this so easy."

"Awww, you make it easy also! I really appreciate you moving in here with me. I know I say it all the time, but I really feel it."

The rest of the week flew by, and after work on Thursday, as they were getting ready to go to the gym, Jason said, "Hey babe, remember my parents are meeting with us this weekend."

"I didn't forget! In fact, Auntie Grace dropped by with some new earrings, and I think they will go great with the outfit that I'm planning to wear."

"Uhhh, OK. Are you planning to dress all indigenous when they come over?"

Nika did a slow head turn to stare at Jason in shock.

"All indigenous? What does that mean?"

Jason could see she was getting upset. "Well, babe," he faltered. "My parents have a tendency to stick their feet into their mouths, and I just think if you come out all decked out in your indigenous stuff, they might say something we will all regret."

"Are you saying your parents are racist?" Nika's voice drops slowly and low.

"NO! NO, GOD, NO." Jason was getting red in the face, and his temper was starting to show through. "I mean, they have no social filter and will say the damnedest things, and I'm trying to do damage control here, Jesus."

"Jason, I'm proud of who I am, this. This is me, this is ME," Nika hits her chest. "I was ashamed of myself for such a long time, and now I am proud of who I am. I am Metis. I am beading and leather. I am feathers and jigging. I am wearing sashes and ribbon skirts. This. Is ME. I'm unapologetically me. I will not apologize, and I will not hide my indigenous spirit because you want to protect your parents. I will not hide; I will not pretend. I'm absolutely hurt and upset that you would ask this of me!"

Nika sat down on the edge of the bed as she started crying.

Jason burst out, "I'm protecting all of you! I just need to ease them into it, into awareness."

"You weren't eased into it."

"Yeah, but I like you. I liked you enough to follow you wherever you take me. I like the bad, the good, all of it."

"Oh, so it's bad."

"NO, god, NO! It's," Jason half screams in frustration. "It's all good, but your history is terrible; what we did was terrible, and sometimes that's hard to hear, hard to know, hard to understand, and I'm not sure they are ready to hear that."

"Well, I don't think my great-grandparents were ready to be starved on the side of the road because of who they were, but that's where we are."

"WOULD YOU LISTEN TO ME?" Jason shouted. "I just want to prevent hurt feelings. That's all I want to do."

"I am listening, and I'm hearing you loud and clear. You want me to hide who I am."

"Just until I can get them to understand."

"Jason, I'm done hiding, and I thought you understood that. I think maybe you'd better leave."

"I'm not leaving."

"Fine then, I'll leave."

"You aren't leaving this house! You have a stalker out there. You need to be careful."

"Then I guess you better leave and maybe spend the night or a few nights at your place. I'm going to go into the bathroom for a bit, and when I come out, I expect you to be gone."

Nika went into the bathroom and locked the door behind her. She could hear Jason grunting angrily as he threw some clothes into his gym bag and stomped down the stairs. She hoped he would leave Bear behind, but she didn't leave the bathroom until she was sure he was gone.

After a while, she heard the door slam, and she ventured out of the bathroom. She went downstairs and found Bear whimpering at the front door. She made sure the alarm was set and then called Bear to join her in the kitchen. She considered making supper, but she had no appetite.

Leaning against the countertop, she found a note on her kitchen island.

"We'll talk later. I'm just looking out for everyone. - Jason."

Nika exploded into sobs. Her heart broke into a million pieces when she thought of how much she had trusted him. She really thought he understood what it took for her to come to a place of pride in her heritage and culture.

She texted Jessie quickly. "Jason and I broke up. I think"

"WHAT! I'm coming right over."

"No, don't bother, I'm a mess."

"NO. I'm on my way."

Nika dropped her phone on the counter and burst into tears again. She really didn't want to have anyone see her right now. But Jessie was always going to be in her corner. So she understood.

She opened a bottle of wine and put two glasses on the countertop, knowing that Jessie would demand a glass for both of them the minute she walked into the house.

Her doorbell rang, and she went over to answer it, knowing that Jessie must have made it in record time.

Sure enough. The teeny blonde bombshell breezed past her and demanded. "Let's open some wine, and you can tell me everything!"

Nika laughed through her tears. "Wine is open and waiting on the kitchen counter." As she locked the door and set the alarm.

Jessie hugged her, and they walked arm-in-arm to the kitchen.

After pouring two glasses and each of them taking a sip, Jessie looked at Nika. "Wanna talk about it?"

"Not really, but we can."

"What happened? Am I going to have to break it off with Cal for you?"

"Oh god, no."

Oh, good, because I don't think I can."

Nika laughed.

"I'm not that petty. Should I be that petty?"

"In the best interests of my dating life: No. No, you should not." Jessie sipped at her wine and waited.

"We were so happy. Things were working so well. He was living here, and Bear was settling in, and we had a routine, and I was so happy!"

"And then?"

"Well, his parents, he wanted me to meet his parents."

"You didn't want to?"

"NO! I did. We were going to have them over this weekend so that they could see his new "digs" even though he still has his apartment, and they were going to meet Bear, too."

"I still think Conall the Bear is the most amazing name."

"Yeah," Nika said, sniffling, "it's so him, it suits him." Nika rubbed the top of his head and took another long sip of her wine.

"Anyways, so his parents were going to come here this weekend, and tonight, as we were getting ready to head to the gym, he reminded me, and I said that I remembered and that Auntie Grace had sent me some new beaded earrings that I think I had just the outfit for."

"Which reminds me", Jessie interrupted. "I need to talk to Auntie Grace about some earrings; she's just the person who can do what I need to be doing. I'm going to that crazy cousin's wedding in two months, and I am going to wear a grape pantsuit. It looks so sharp, but a pair of Grace's earrings would seal the deal. I need to send her a picture of the suit so she knows what to do. She's so talented. I keep interrupting! Sorry! Keep going."

Nika laughed. "Grace has the best sense of style. Sooo. Jason asks me if I am going to "Dress all indigenous" when they come over."

Jessie exploded. "HE DID WHAT?"

Nika nodded her head. "Yeah, he said he was protecting me and them because they have no social filter, and he wanted to ease them into my indigeneity."

"Excuse me?!? What the fuck just happened!? Are they racist?"

"I know, right? Like I asked him the same thing, and he got so mad. He was like No, they aren't racist, but they needed to be eased into it. I was so hurt and mad, I asked him to pack some things and leave."

"Serves him right!"

"So he left me this note about protecting me," and left. Nika shows Jessie the note.

"I'm so sorry, babe."

"Yeah, so I think we're done. I can't live with someone who asks me to hide who I am just so that he can let his parents be comfortable with what they think I am."

"No, and if he knew anything about your culture and history, he would know that repressing and denying your lineage is a huge sore point for you."

"Right? So much for a woke person." Nika shook her head and took another big sip of her glass. "God, I feel like such a big idiot."

"You're not, you know, you opened yourself up to an experience that was wonderful for a while." Jessie finished her glass. "Want me to spend the night?"

"No, no, I'll be OK."

"Because I can." She walked over to the sink and put her glass in it. As she collected her keys and wallet, she hugged Nika one last time. "Look, we'll be fine. We'll weather this. It's always us two together against the world, OK? See you tomorrow at work, and don't forget to lock the door."

"Yes, I will." She walked Jessie out of the house, standing on her front porch as she watched her get into her car, and then she went back inside to lock up and set the alarm.

She poured the rest of the bottle into her wine glass and called Bear as she trudged back up to the bathroom to take a long, hot bath with her wine and her dog. She may not be crying anymore, but she was sure she just broke her heart. It hurt so much to think of what happened tonight.

Maybe tomorrow would be better. At least she would have the luxury of work to keep her occupied for most of the day. She closed her eyes and tried to focus on her breathing, anything really, so as not to think about the events of this evening. It was going to be a long, rough night.

Chapter 19

Early the next morning, she woke up with gritty eyes from all the crying. She vaguely remembered Bear barking at something at about 3 am. But by the time she woke up enough to look into it, Bear had stopped barking. She raced around the house and realized that Jason wouldn't be there at noon to take Bear out, so she packed him up and brought him into the office with her. It may take some fast talking on her part to get Terrell on her side, but there was that girl on the 3 floor who brought her emotional support dog to work, so maybe she could get a pass for the next few days.

The trip into the office with Bear in the car was stressful; he didn't understand what was happening, and he almost peed on her car seat. But when they got to the office, all the "ooooo" and "ahhhhh's more than made up for everything. Everyone already seemed to know what was going on. Jessie had forewarned Terrell, who had, of course, told his work wife Nancy, who had a tendency to be a bit of a work gossip, and the word spread like wildfire from there.

Nika popped into Terrell's office, bringing Bear with her. "Hey, Terrell, this is Bear, and he's still too young to leave at home all day, Jason and I….," Nika trailed off as she sniffled.

"Hey Nika, no worries," Terrell interrupted. "Jessie told me all about it. Damn shame, huh? He looked so good right up to that."

Terrell came around his desk and crouched down to give Bear some scratches and snuggles. "I'm sure this bad boy will be more than welcome; you may find people in the office coming to borrow him for snuggles occasionally."

"Thanks, boss, for understanding. I promise that as soon as I can leave him at home, I will do that. Thank you for understanding that I am just not ready to talk about what happened yet," her eyes reddened from repressed tears. "You'd think I'd be used to people letting me down, but I just had so much hope for this one." She looked away to hold back the tears that were threatening to spill over.

"I get it. I did some pretty clueless and hurtful stuff to my wife when we were dating, and I've been fully schooled in empathy and sympathy."

"Thanks, Terrell, and thank your wife for me, too. She's a real treasure."

Terrell laughed. "Just you wait. She's making you sympathy muffins, a feel-better treat."

"Oh well," Terrell's wife was not a good baker, and everyone had suffered from her baking at some point, but as Terrell liked to remind them, it was done with love. "That's beautiful of her. I'll just remember to share them with the office."

Terrell groaned. "You're going to get me killed. If not by my wife, then by the team."

Nika laughed as she walked back to her office. She set Bear up on the floor beside her desk with his bed, chew toys, and breakfast. She hung his leash on her coat hook so she wouldn't be scrambling to find it when he needed to go out for a potty break. She shut her door to her office with a sign outside letting everyone know that there was a dog inside and to please knock before entering. Then she got down to work.

Not even 20 minutes later, Jessie came breezing into her office.

"I thought I put a sign up to knock?"

"Oh, you did, but Conall knows me. Don't you, honeybuns." She scooched down on the floor so that the dog could crawl into her lap for snuggles.

"How are you doing?"

Nika sighed. She really didn't want to discuss this. "I'm doing fine. A bit headachey from all the crying."

"And the wine."

Nika shook her head. "And the wine," she agreed. "I'm thinking I'll stop going to the gym even though I will miss it. That's Jason's space and not mine."

"NO, ABSOLUTELY NOT. I'll talk to Cal, and we will figure out something. You aren't giving up the things you have grown to love just because your ex is a putz."

Nika stiffened at the word ex. Was Jason an ex? Was this the end? She had been grieving him like it was the end, but to hear it put like that was jarring. Was she ready to walk away from him? How do you give someone who hurt you like that the opportunity to come back? What if it happened again?

Nika nodded. "OK. You talk to Cal, and if you two can find a way that I won't have to see or deal with Jason, then I'll meet you there. But I'm serious. I don't really want to run into him. I'm really hurt and mad. I can't see his face right now."

"Noted. "Jessie nodded. "Are you guys really over?"

"I think so. I mean, it was a pretty big deal, and I just can't forget it and pretend he didn't ask that of me. But I'll be honest, when you called him my ex, I was not prepared for that."

"Got it."

She sniffled a bit. "I really thought he was the one."

Jessie stood up and hugged her. "Then maybe you aren't done yet, but Jason needs to fix this, not you."

"Yes, you are right."

With that, Jessie walked out of her office, saying, "I'll keep you updated on what Cal says!"

"Thanks, Jessie!"

Nika put her head down and got to work. She knew that using the time to concentrate on other things would be good for her. She soon lost herself in the numbers, only coming up for air at lunch to take Bear on a quick walk around the downtown area. Then, there was a quick lunch with Jessie, where they talked about boring client accounts for a change. By 3 pm, she wasn't sure where the day had gone, but she was grateful for the distraction.

Jessie texted her, "Hey, Cal is going to ask Jason if he wants anything from your house, and if you can bring it to the gym, Cal will give it to him. You and I are going to work out in another part of the gym with those girls we keep watching. They look like they are having fun all the time, remember? Well, Cal reached out to one and asked if we could join for a bit while we figure out some things. He's going to lift with Jason and maybe try to get some sense into his head. Cal's super embarrassed about Jason's response on your behalf, but he also knows Jason is stubborn, especially when he's sure he was doing the right thing. I'll miss my big teddy bear, but it'll be great. OK?"

"OK, get me that list, and I'll pack it up before I head to the gym. Thank you, Jessie, and thank Cal, for me."

"Hey babe, no problem, you know I always have your back."

Chapter 20

Nika rushed home after the long work day and collected the items that Jason had requested through Cal, who sent them through Jessie. She really appreciated the lengths her friends were going through to make sure she felt protected and comfortable with this new reality. She hurriedly dressed in her gym gear and put Bear in his kennel. She wanted to get to the gym first and get amongst that group of women before Jason even knew she was there. Jessie had told her that Cal was going to let Jason assume that they had picked up the gear before going to the gym and not tell him that she was at the gym working out, too. Maybe she was being cowardly, and hopefully, over time, she wouldn't feel this overwhelming need to hide from him, but right now, she felt fragile and weak and was grateful her friends would let her lean on them until she found her emotional footing again.

She ate a quick carb snack, and every little bit of this routine reminded her of some of the happiest days of her life. She was really regretful of how well their lives fit together and how much she was actually turning her back on with the end of this relationship. Jason had made her better. He had changed her, unfortunately, right now. That just felt like a one-way street.

She walked into the gym and immediately looked over at the squat racks where she, Jason, Jessie, and Cal would hang out. She saw Cal setting up, and no sign of Jason, so she waved at him and dropped her gym bag on the floor. She pointed to the box in her hand. Cal pointed at the group of women over to the left of the gym and gave her a thumbs-up. Stacey, a girl she had met last week, popped her head up in the group and waved her over. Picking up her gym bag, she headed over to them. Stacey met her halfway and grabbed the box, "This is the jerk's stuff?"

"Jerk?"

"Cal told us the short version of what happened. That's not cool. Jason is a great guy, but that was a classic jerk move. He's going to have to make this right. He's a jerk until then."

"I didn't really want to take his friends away from him." She wrung her hands.

"Hey, honey, my sister is married to a black man. It's hard, it's SO hard, watching them navigate the world of race so carefully and then hear Jason say something like what he said to you. It changes things. It changes a lot of things!"

"OK. Thank you for letting me join you. I don't know how good I will be, but I'll try. You guys always look so intense and difficult!"

"Oh, don't worry about that. It's not easy, not even for me, not even now, and my lord, when I started, I had two left feet, and I couldn't do half the moves at all. I've watched you with Jason and Cal, and I know both you and Jessie will start out a little further ahead of where I started. You'll be fine, but be ready to sweat!"

"Got it."

Jessie waltzed into the gym and skipped over to Cal to give him a big kiss before running to join the group. Stacey was still holding the box, so she offered to run it over to Cal. As she did that, Jessie pulled her into the group huddle. "I think I saw Jason pulling up, so let's get in the middle of this mess so he doesn't notice us."

"What will happen if he asks Cal where you are?"

"Cal's going to be honest and tell him that I'm over here because I'm mad at him. So maybe sit a few people away from me so he doesn't see you."

Nika shook her head in assent.

The women brought her into the circle and started hugging her with a chorus of "We heard what happened." "We got you," and "How are you doing?"

She was so grateful to have found these people through Jason and, once again, for the millionth time, wondered how he could be such a great guy and be so wrong at the same time. Maybe there was hope that the great guy could realize exactly how he had made her feel.

Those women worked hard. She was left gasping and sweating on the floor after they completed the circuit, with Jessie lying there with her. They joked and ribbed around with the other women, and during the whole workout, there was a chilly silence radiating towards Jason all night. Nika stole a quick peek at him during their workout, and he looked terrible. It was as if he hadn't slept all night. He and Cal were talking in short, terse words and quietly doing their workout, the boisterous, almost obnoxious energy of past workouts definitely missing. Suddenly, Stacey stood up. "OK, ladies, he's gone." Everyone stretched and got up. Nika peeked to see Cal heading towards Jessie. He crouched down beside them and said, "I don't know how many times we can do this before he figures it out, but it worked tonight."

Jessie smiled softly at him, "I could do this all the time. I think I've found my people!"

"Me too," Nike piped up. "But I don't expect y'all to make arrangements to hide me from him all the time, just until I'm a bit stronger and more capable of dealing with whatever his stubborn self throws at me."

"I talked to him a bit tonight," Cal said. "He's a wreck, but he still insists he's right. I told him that I didn't agree with him on that, but he's definitely hurting too. It's not just you."

"Thanks, Cal, you didn't have to do that."

"No, I did have to tell him that. I like you, but more than that, he's my friend, and he is HAPPY with you. He was completely over the moon about dating you in ways I have never seen him. He needs to understand that he hurt you, in order for you two to figure this out. He still doesn't quite see it. I know what the problem is, other than he's incredibly stubborn, he's letting his privilege stand in the way right now and as a result he can't meet you where you are, and if he can't compromise to meet you in the middle, he's not working hard enough at being a good partner. We'll get there, I think. He's a good guy, and he means well. But as much as he would go to the ends of the earth for you, he would protect his mom and dad equally as much, and I think he was afraid they would do or say something by accident that would create a chasm he couldn't cross. He wanted to "manage" it as much as he could. Unfortunately, his solutions really hurt your feelings."

"I get that, Cal, but he asked me to repress who I am so he could have the luxury of affording them that comfort while learning."

"And that was wrong. I know it was SO wrong, but he's not there yet. I'll get through to him."

"It's not our job to educate him. It's his job."

"No, but it's my job as a friend to encourage him to keep learning and doing everything he can to increase his awareness of his privilege and how that affects his perception."

Jessie interrupted. "I don't know about you two, but I'm going to drag myself out of here and go and have a hot bath."

Cal grinned. "Care to have me join you?"

"Ohhh yeah, that would be nice, that would be very nice."

Nika felt a sharp pain at their togetherness; she really missed having Jason's arms around her while she listened to them. "You two go home," she laughed. "I'm going to stay here dead."

Stacey laughed and dragged her up by the arm. "Oh no, chica, you are going home. We're shutting down, and you are going home."

Cal looked at her. "I promised Jason I would look out for you. You still have someone out there doing some pretty weird things, so I'm going to walk you out to your car and make sure you get in it safely."

She bit her lip and nodded her head.

Chapter 21

Jessie, Cal, and she walked out to their vehicles, all conveniently parked in the same place. Cal quickly checked both her and Jessie's back seats and watched her get in the car and drive away. Jessie and he headed back home to Jessie's place.

Unaware of the car and truck following her home, Nika blared the tunes while she drove home, looking forward to an evening just snuggling with her pup.

Jason followed her in his truck, and he knew she was at the gym. He had noticed her car in the parking lot but had chosen to respect her obvious need for space. He couldn't just leave it at that, though. He needed to follow her home and make sure she made it home safely before he went home. He didn't notice the dark blue car also following Nika's home and failed to notice when that car parked halfway down the block from her place. Jason watched her pull into her driveway and slowed down to make sure she got into the door safely. Once she shut the door, he headed back to his empty apartment. Why couldn't she understand he was trying to be fair to everyone?

As he pulled into his apartment complex parking lot, his phone buzzed. Looking down at it, he saw his mom's number. He sighed. He was dreading this call. He put the truck in park and grabbed the phone.

"Hey, Ma."

"Hi, Sweetie. Your father and I were just talking about how excited we were to meet your new flame this weekend. I was just calling to ask if we should bring anything. Wine? Does she drink?"

"Uhhh yeah, Mom, it's been called off."

"What? Why? What happened?"

"We had a fight, and I'm not staying with her anymore."

"WHAT? But you were so happy! What happened? Tell me all about it."

"Nah, Ma, it just didn't work out."

"But what about her stalker and all that?"

"Well, I still drive by and check on her."

"Are you the stalker?"

"WHAT? MA! NO! JEEZ. Did you raise me to be that kind of guy?"

"Well, no, but I also didn't raise you to have 5 bazillion tattoos, and look what I have now."

"MA, Jesus Christ." He took a deep breath. "We had some fundamental differences that came out in an argument. And we decided to take a break; however, I think we're done."

"I'm sorry, honey, I was really looking forward to meeting this young woman. You haven't sounded that happy in a long time."

"I know, Ma, I'm sorry too. I gotta go in and shower. I just got home from the gym, and I'm sitting in the cab of my truck, stinking it up, talking to you."

"Go home, son, and your father and I will talk to you later. We love you."

"Love you too, Ma. Give my best to Dad."

He hung up and banged his head on the steering wheel in frustration a few times. This just really, really sucked.

Grabbing his gear, he headed into the apartment building. He didn't notice the car slowly pull out of the parking spot down the street and do a U-turn to head back to Nika's house. He didn't notice much of anything. He just wanted a hot shower and a cold beer to soothe the sting.

Chapter 22

Nika spent the rest of the evening just playing with Bear and relaxing. She put on a true crime documentary in the background, but quickly realized that it likely wasn't the smartest thing to be listening to when she had a potential stalker.

She opted for another long hot bath with Epsom salts to manage the muscle tightness that the workout Stacey had led was now giving her. How could one tiny woman be such a drill sergeant? She didn't know, but she was going to hurt tomorrow, and she could already feel it. She grabbed a cold glass of water and cajoled Bear to come upstairs. Placing his bed in the bathroom, she poured a bath and grabbed her book to relax for a bit before bedtime.

Her bath was so relaxing that it took her virtually no time to fall asleep once she crawled into bed.

She woke up at 2 am to Bear frantically barking.

"BEAR! What is it?"

She turned on her lamp and found him scratching at the door frantically.

"Do you need to go out?"

Suddenly, she heard her alarm go off. She sat straight up in her bed and reached for her phone. Her hands shook as she dialed 911.

"911, please state your emergency."

"My name is Nika Dorion, and I think my house is being broken into. My house alarm just went off, and my dog was frantically barking and scratching at my bedroom door before the alarm went off. I also need you to know I'm legally deaf, so I won't hear you very well, if at all."

The operator asked for her address and told her to remain calm.

"I've dispatched the police to come to your place. You don't use a TTY?"

"No, Smartphones manage almost everything I need. I never anticipated needing 911. Thank you."

"No worries, we will muddle through. Just stay on the line until the police get there." The operator continued to ask questions, but it was getting harder and harder to hear her, with Bear barking madly and scratching at the door. Finally, the operator said really loudly. "LOCK YOUR DOOR!" Nika gasped and ran to the door, locking it quickly.

Seconds later, she saw the door handle turn, and when it wouldn't open, she could see whoever was in the house start to jiggle it. "GET OUT OF MY HOUSE. THE POLICE ARE ON THE WAY!" she screamed.

This jiggling stopped, but Bear continued to bark wildly. The operator tried to get Nika to calm down enough to tell her what was going on. "Someone's trying to open my door!" She sobbed. "They keep jiggling the knob."

"Just stay right there. I've told the police that it's an active break-in and the perpetrator is still in the house. They are about 3 minutes away."

"I can't hear you. Just please get here fast."

"We're doing the best we can. Do not engage with the perpetrator."

Nika ran from her bed, grabbed Bear, ran into the bathroom, and locked the door. Sobbing loudly, she said, "I just ran into my bathroom and locked that door, too. Now they have two locked doors to get through."

The operator said something, but Nika couldn't make any sense of it. The panic had settled in too well, muddying up any chance she had of making sense of anything she was "hearing."

Suddenly, the operator said really loudly. "THE POLICE ARE THERE, AND THE HOUSE IS EMPTY. CAN YOU UNLOCK THE DOORS AND LET THEM TALK TO YOU?"

"Oh, oh yes!"

Nika unlocked the bathroom door and ran to the bedroom door to unlock it swiftly. Two police officers were on the other end. She recognized the one from the prior visit.

"Hey! Where's your friend?" he asked.

"We broke up."

"Aww, shame to hear that. But I see you still have that cute dog. Can I take that phone from you and talk to the dispatcher for a second?"

Nika handed him the phone while the other officer walked around her room, making sure they were alone.

Once he hung up, the officer looked at her seriously. "OK, well, someone definitely broke into your house, and we can see that they tried to break into your bedroom. I am going to recommend you stay somewhere else tonight. You gotta friend you can call?"

"Uhhh, yes. I can text Jessie and spend the night with her."

She took her phone back from him and started texting Jessie. Since Jessie and she worked together, they could head in together in the morning, so Nika just packed up what she needed, and the police offered to drop her off at Jessie's place.

Once there, they snuggled up under a blanket and watched Bear play with a toy while they had a glass of wine and discussed the events. It didn't take long for them to get sleepy again. Nika camped out on the couch and tried to sleep as best as she could.

Chapter 23

The next morning, she woke up to several texts from people. Jessie had phoned and texted several people while Nika was sleeping. Cal was offering to go over to her house and make sure the door and alarm system were OK. She was going to take him up on that. Jessie suggested that since Cal had a key to her place, Nika could just leave her keys on the counter, and Cal would swing by and pick them up. Her mom and aunts all texted, wanting to know if she was OK and if she wanted to get out of town for a few days and go to any of their homes. She turned them all down. She just wanted to get back to her normalcy as fast as possible. A normalcy that was slowly shrinking away, and she felt desperate to grab onto it and hold it as tight as possible. Terrell had texted, saying that she didn't have to come into the office today. She texted him back, letting him know that she was still coming in, and she needed the distraction.

The police had called her, likely with an update. She had Jessie listen to the message, and she called the number back on speakerphone, leaving a message informing the officer that she preferred text if at all possible. Jessie sat on her couch, drinking her morning coffee, waiting while Nika finished her last-minute details before they headed to work. She patted the seat beside her, and Nika sat down, knowing that a difficult conversation was coming up.

"Nika, Cal wants to tell Jason."

"Why?"

"Well, some of his stuff is still there, and he should likely go and see if anything is missing. Cal could potentially use his help with some repairs. However, Cal will be very careful and make sure that Jason is gone before you come home. OK?"

"I can't argue with any of that. I want to, though, you know, it just feels like an extra layer of violation that I have to let him into my house when I'm not there to protect it, but I know he wouldn't do anything. I just feel completely bombarded with violations."

Jessie wrapped her free arm around Nika's shoulders and half-hugged her. "I know, I know. But let's let the boys do their thing."

"OK, Fine.. I will text Cal and tell him he has my approval to do that. He should have it in a text that I'm allowing him to bring my ex into my home. It should come from me; there's probably some legal requirement or something like that."

Jessie nodded and took a sip of her coffee. Nika texted Cal as they headed into the office. "Hey, I know Jason needs to know. Jessie and I discussed it, and I realized he still needs to check on his things in my home. I would rather he were there when I wasn't there, so I will give you permission to let him in the house while you do repairs. I know you could probably use his help."

"Thanks, Nika. He'll be gone before you get home."

"Thanks Cal. You are good people."

"So are you. He cares about you, Nika, a lot. More than I've ever seen him care about anyone, and he fucked up, but I like to think he's going to make it right because that's the person I'm friends with."

"I hope he does too, Cal. I miss him, but I have to hold the line for this one. I just hope he gets it before it's too late for us to come back to an understanding. I really thought he was my forever person."

"Me too. Tell Jessie I love her, and I'll see her tonight."

"OHHHHH, you said the L WORD?!"

"Uhh, Jessie didn't tell you? Well shit, look at the time I gotta go!"

Nika craned her neck right around Exorcist style to stare at her best friend.

"Jessie," she said in a serious tone.

"Mhmm?" Jessie said, taking her eyes off the road to look at Nika. "OH MY GOD WHAT NOW?"

"Cal said to tell you he loves you." Nika's voice dropped down into her voice of doom.

Jessie's eyes pop wide open. "I MEANT TO TELL YOU!! I DID, I DID! There's just been so much happening for you!"

"Ohmygod, that is no excuse! I am always happy for you, and I always want to hear your good news. So what happened? I finally get to say it! DEETS! NOW! Wait, does Terrell know?"

"Does Terrell know? Why would I tell our boss?"

"Even better now, I get to put you in front of him like you did me."

"OH MY GOD. You wouldn't! It was an accident!"

Nika grinned at her evilly.

Jessie broke out in laughter. "OK, I deserve that. But still. You wanted details?"

"Always." Trying for a British accent like Alan Rickman.

Jessie busted out laughing again. "OK, Jeeze you can be terrifying, you know that?"

She took a deep breath, and her eyes softened as she watched the road. "It was so romantic, Nika, like you with Jason. I'm really starting to think he may be the one." She glanced over at Nika to see her smiling a big smile back and nodding. "So we were having dinner after our workout, and we were talking about growing up and our respective families. Suddenly, he just stopped and stared at me. So, you know me, I get super paranoid, and I said, "What?! Do I have something in my teeth?" And he laughed and said, "No, I was just struck by how beautiful you are and how happy I am just being around you." I just about died. I blushed; you know I blush over the slightest things, so I blushed really red. He grabbed my hand, rubbed the top of my hand with his thumb, and pulled me into his lap." Jessie took a breath, and Nika yelled, "Don't stop! You're just getting to the good part!"

"OK! Let me take a breath, woman! So I'm sitting in his lap, and he's rubbing my thigh, and he says. "I love you, Jessie Jane." And by god, I really regretted my mom and dad for their naming choices right then because I busted out laughing."

"YOU DID NOT."

"I DID! I grabbed him, kissed him hard, and said, 'I love you too, but let's not name our kids Jessie Jane, Charlie Chuck, or Amanda Anne, OK?"

"Oh, lord, Jessie."

"He laughed and agreed."

"Talking about kids already?"

"Well, didn't you and Jason?"

"No, we never got that far." Nika smiled sadly. "Too much going on, you know."

"Yeah."

"Anyways, you said the big L! I'm fantastically happy for you!"

Chapter 24

They chattered animatedly as they made their way into the office. Terrell popped his head out while they were making their way to their offices. "Hey, Nika, could I talk to you?"

"Sure thing, Terrell."

She dropped everything off in her office, set up Bear, and made her way to Terrell's office.

"You wanted to talk to me, boss?"

"Sit down," as he closed the door. Nika sobered up, realizing that this wasn't going to be a fun conversation.

"I wanted to take the time to let you know that we are fully supportive of anything you need to get your life figured out. If you need to take time off, get out of town, and see your mom or your family, we will support it. I can't imagine how stressful this is, and I'm not sure the added stress of work would be helpful."

"Actually, Terrell, I'm finding work the least of my stresses, and it helps me to disconnect and get distracted from everything that's happening. If you don't want me here because you feel I pose a risk to the organization."

"Absolutely not! I just don't want you to feel like this job would put any pressure on you to be here if that's not helping in any way. I talked to the team about workloads and people having room to take on a few things should you need to step away for a bit." He stood up and came around the desk to lean against it in front of her as he talked.

"Annie and I were talking about it last night, and she said if this were happening to her, she would want to go home and be with her parents and just get out of town. So I thought maybe that would be something you might want to do." Terrell patted her on the shoulder carefully.

"I wouldn't want to bring this to my mom. Whatever this is. No, Terrell, I appreciate the support and the understanding, but until further notice, I will be coming into work."

"OK, but let me know if any of it is getting to be too much."

"Sure thing, I can promise to do that. But hey, did you know Jessie said the big L word to her hunk of love?"

Terrell popped up. "WHAAAA? Why am I always the last to know?"

"I just found out myself. She was keeping it down low because of "all your stuff," she said. Looks like we need to do another karaoke night and invite Cal for 20 questions."

"Yes, we do!"

"My work here is done."

Nika made her way to her office with a little smirk on her face. Throwing herself into her work was satisfying, only to come up for air on her break to listen to Jessie bitch her out for telling Terrell. They made tentative plans with Terrell to get the gang together on Friday for drinks at the local pub, and this time, Cal would be in the hot seat. Nika laughingly left the two of them planning the event with a comment, "I'm still not singing karaoke!" and went back to her office to let Bear out for a potty break.

Later that afternoon, Cal texted her to let her know that everything was repaired at her place. She thanked him again and told him to thank Jason for her. He agreed to pass the message on. Her heart hurt, her head hurt, but deep down, she knew she was doing the right thing.

Again, the week dragged at an agonizing pace and yet so very fast. She continued to bring Bear to work, and Jessie and Cal checked on her routinely. They all met at the gym regularly. Stacey was becoming a close friend and confidant as well, and the other women giving Jason the stink eye made her heart feel full and a little guilty.

Friday finally finished with a sense of relief. Her cousin Gabe dropped by late Thursday night, begging for a place to sleep for the weekend while he went to a concert with a lady friend. Personally, she was sure he was just looking out for her at the auntie's bequest, but she agreed to let him spend the weekend. As a result, she left Bear with him on Friday while she went to work so that she could go to the pub with her work friends and have the pleasure of grilling Cal in front of Jessie. The evening was a good time, something she really needed in the face of all this stress and worry. Cal and Jessie trailed her home and made sure she got into the house safely while Gabe waved at them from the front door. She felt a bit like an escorted prisoner, but she knew everyone cared. If she was honest, she was grateful for the company. It had been difficult sleeping in her house alone since that terrifying night, and having Gabe around let her indulge in a full night of sleep for a change. They spent most of Friday night chatting and visiting, Gabe telling her all about this girl he was seeing and his university classes. She shared her heartbreak with him about Jason, and although Gabe seemed a bit off about it, it made her wonder if she was overreacting after all.

"Hey, Gabe?" She called out while he was in the living room.

He peeked his head around the corner.

"Yeah?"

"Do you think I'm too hard on Jason?"

"Oh, hell no."

"Then what's up?"

Gabe ran his fingers through his hair and sighed. "Look, cuz. All I know is that man loved you like a full-on deer in headlights loved you. Frozen in his spot. And I get that he fucked up. Like he fuccccked up." Gabe drawled out the words long and slow. "I'm a little disappointed that he's not apologized yet because he really needs to for you both to move on, and I get that he's stubborn, but the dude full-on loves you, not loved, this isn't a past tense, one and done, move off into the sunset kind of love. It's the he loves you and will never get enough of loving you kind of love. It was the kind of love you see in Ma and Pa's eyes. He had that look."

Nika's eyes welled up. "Yeah," she said softly.

"Hey!" Gabe moved in and hugged her tight. "I know your battles, I get it, you're struggling with if you are worth it, but cuz you are worth him walking through the fires of hell and back. OK? This isn't about you sticking to your guns. This is completely about him not seeing the forest for the trees. And honestly, cuz I think he will figure it out. I am 100% sure he will. He just needs to hurry it up a little before you lose all faith." Gabe wiped away the tears and hugged her again.

He reiterated. "You are worth everything and all the things that he has to do to show he's up to the task of being with you."

"That big a problem, huh?" Nika laughed through the tears.

"Oh, cousin, you have no idea what he's getting himself into. Between you and Jessie, oh man, he's in for a wild ride he will never recover from until he's on his deathbed."

Nika laughed a full belly laugh at that.

"Thanks, Gabe. I needed that. I'm exhausted and going to bed."

"Night, cousin, see you in the morning."

Chapter 25

The next morning, it dawned bright and early. Nika was feeling super hemmed in, so she decided to take a walk or jog around the neighborhood with Bear.

She bounded down the stairs and quietly made some coffee while Gabe still slept. She debated leaving him a note while she and Bear went out, but suddenly, she heard the guest room door open and Gabe clomp down the stairs clumsily.

"Hey, princess!" she called out. "Want some coffee?"

Gabe stumbled into the kitchen, nodding his head yes while rubbing his eyes.

He said to her, "You look ready to take on the world."

She laughed, "I was thinking of going for a jog with Bear," she signed back. It was rare that she signed, but having Gabe here reminded her of home and growing up in the kitchen with her Kokum, hands furiously flying with stories and love.

"Gimme a second," He signed, "I'll come. I need the fresh air."

"OK, you've got 5 minutes, dude! I'll be ready to go after my cup of coffee."

Gabe raced back upstairs and changed into some grey sweats and a T-shirt. Grabbing his phone, he winced, still tired from the evening before. But he couldn't let Nika run alone. This was going to be rough.

They jogged around the neighborhood in companionable silence, Bear enjoying the fresh air while he kept up on his sturdy legs.

Once done, they devoured a hearty breakfast, and Gabe went up to shower while she sat in the living room working on a beading project she decided to start for her Christmas gift to her Kokum.

The doorbell rang. She wasn't expecting anyone, so she curiously got up and went to the door. Peeking outside, she saw a tall, willowy older woman and a shorter man standing behind her.

She opened the door hesitantly. "Hi?"

"Are you Nika?"

"Yes? And you are?"

"Oh yes, I'm Dottie, and this is my husband, Roger. Roger say Hi."

Behind her, he quietly rumbles, "Hi"

"Hi, Dottie and Roger, pleased to meet you, but that still doesn't tell me who you are."

"Oh yes!" Dottie laughed. "Silly me. We're Jason's parents."

Nika stood back, stunned.

"Excuse me, what?"

"We're Jason's parents, and I'm here to understand why you are no longer dating my son. May we come in?"

Roger stared at the back of his wife's head. "Now, darling, that sounded really threatening. Why don't you tone it down a bit?"

"Oh!" Dottie gasped. "I didn't mean it like that. I'm just very forthright, as the boys and Roger like to tell me."

Nika noticed her neighbor's curtain twitching and knew that she would be over in about 10 minutes to "make sure she was OK" if she didn't let these two people into her house. She opened the door and gestured for them to come in.

"Please, why don't you come in? I'll make you a cup of coffee while we talk about this."

"Thank you, dear."

Dottie and Roger came into her house and immediately started looking around.

"You have a beautiful home," Dottie exclaimed.

"Thank you," said Nika. Dottie homed in on the beading on the coffee table.

"Did you do that?"

"Yes, it's a gift for my Kokum."

Roger turned to look at her. "Your what?"

Nika looked him square in the eye. "My kokum, it means grandmother."

"Ah," said Roger, nodding thoughtfully.

She led them into the kitchen and invited them to sit down while she made them each a cup of coffee.

"Does Jason know you are here?"

"Absolutely not. That boy would be furious."

"Why are you here then?" Nika asked.

"Jason was so happy to tell us that he was dating you. He had a twinkle in his voice when he would tell us all about you."

"A twinkle in his voice?"

"Well, yes. We haven't seen much of him since he started dating you because he was dating you. But when he called to chat, he was happy, so very happy, and it made my heart full. Then you two broke up, and he's miserable. I can hear it in his voice and see it in his eyes every time he comes over. As a mother, I need to help fix that."

"Y-You can't really fix your son's mistakes."

"Oh, so it was his mistake."

Gabe came bounding down the stairs, toweling his hair dry. He stopped and stared at Dottie and Roger while they stared back.

"Hey, cousin," he signed. "You OK?"

She signed "Yes."

Dottie looked at Gabe. "Are you deaf?"

He shook his head no. "But Nika is," he said.

Dottie gasped. "What? But she's talking to us."

"I said she was deaf, not mute." Gabe grinned.

Roger laughed, "Kid's gotta point, Dottie."

"Gabe, this is Dottie and Roger, Jason's folks." Gabe's eyes widened in sudden understanding. "Dottie and Roger, this is my cousin Gabe. He's been spending a couple of days with me since my house was broken into on Tuesday night."

"Oh my goodness, you need Jason back here right now!" Dottie exclaimed.

Nika was a little taken aback at how quickly Dottie would put her son in the line of danger.

"It's dangerous being a woman alone. You need someone strong and capable." Dottie insisted.

"Thanks for that," muttered Gabe.

Nika shook her head. "I'm not ready to do that just yet, Dottie."

Gabe interrupted. "If you are OK, I'm going to head out back to the farm and check on Ma and Kokum. Pa is out hunting right now."

"You're stretched too thin, Gabe. I'll be fine. Give my love to Auntie and Kokum."

Roger interrupted, "OK OK, you told me Kokum means grandmother, but what language is that, is it Greek?"

Gabe said simply, "Metis."

"Oh, so you are Indian."

Gabe's smile got a little frosty. "We accept Indigenous, but we prefer Metis."

"Got it, kid. I'm just asking questions." Roger replied kindly.

Gabe relaxed and stared at Nika. She shrugged back. She was starting to see what had Jason worried, but she knew she still had to hold the line and trust that she was doing the right thing. It seemed to her that in spite of Jason's well founded worries, his parents were up to the task of navigating things proactively.

He reached in and kissed the side of her cheek, "Show Ma your beading. She would love it. You bead almost as well as she does."

"I will, I promise."

Bear slowly sauntered into the kitchen and flopped down on the rug beside her feet.

Dottie looked at the big puppy and said, "That's a beautiful dog. What is it?"

Nika watched her intently as she said, "Pitbull, Gabe breeds them and gave me the best of the litter when it became apparent I had unwanted attention. Can I ask how you know where I live?"

Dottie relaxed. "Oh, that's easy. Jason gave us your address when we thought we were coming over for dinner. But then things fell through."

"Oh, that makes sense."

Dottie put her coffee mug down after a sip and tried to be nonchalant. "So, did Jason screw up with your deafness or your Metisness? Is that a word?"

Nika just about spat out her coffee.

Dottie continued on, "I'm not here to waste time. I want to get to the bottom of this, and frankly, Jason, god love him, can be a bit of a bulldog when he thinks he's right and knowing you are deaf and Metis, I figure those are two areas he doesn't have a lot of expertise in and could make some mistakes. "

"Now, Dottie." Roger began. "If she doesn't want to tell us, then we aren't going to push. Remember?"

Dottie looked at Nika expectantly.

Nika put down her coffee mug on the table and sat down with them. "Jason," she took a deep breath. "Loves you both very, very much."

Dottie quietly muttered, "Oh dear."

"He asked me not to dress all indigenous when you came over because he wanted to protect you from making a mistake."

Roger and Dottie sat back, stunned. Finally, she exploded.

"The nerve of that boy," she yelled. "I don't know if I should be mad at him on your behalf or on ours. We're not dumb, you know, we can learn."

"He wanted to ease you both into it, and my people have been repressed and asked to culturally deny ourselves for far too long for me to agree to that. So we had a fight. I can't back down from this, Dottie, no matter how much I love him."

"You love him, though."

"Desperately. If one thing this space we're giving each other has taught me is that I love him desperately, he's my other person. But I won't sacrifice my self-respect for love. As much as I want to, I can't do that."

"We understand, dear. Right, Roger?"

"Absolutely, we love our son and want the best for him, but we'll have your back on this."

"Beautifully said, dear." Dottie gazed at him with much love. Nika's heart almost hurt to see it. She wanted that, and when she looked at Jason, she saw the potential for that.

"I just don't understand how he was so naturally accepting of me, and both of you seem so easygoing. Why was he worried?"

Dottie laughed. Roger coughed and looked at his wife. "Shall I take this one?" Dottie was still laughing, so she nodded.

"It's easy, really sweetie." Roger started to explain as Nika stiffened up slightly at the "sweetie comment." "I am not always politically correct, and sometimes I can come off as too familiar or ignorant because I'll just say whatever I think. Dottie, if you haven't noticed, will get right to the point with no social filter."

Nika nodded her head thoughtfully. Roger continued on. "We always mean well, but frankly, we've put our feet in it more than once. I'm sure he was just trying to make sure that our meeting went as smoothly as possible."

Dottie nodded thoughtfully and joined in. "Sometimes I wonder if our boys feel the need to constantly manage our social interactions with their other loved ones. I've caught Devin, Jason's older brother, wincing from time to time when I'm talking with his wife, and I've learned that then is a good time to shut up and ask her if I'm causing any problems. We aren't here to make their lives more difficult, but I suspect sometimes we do." Dottie patted Rogers' hand.

"Don't be afraid to tell us when we are making mistakes. We've become very adept at taking constructive criticism." Roger piped up, "And we will make mistakes. I'm always saying something I shouldn't or thinking some joke is appropriate, and whoops, no, it's not."

"But you mean well," Nika said softly while nodding. "Absolutely," Roger said.

"Should we tell Jason to get his head on straight?" Dottie asked.

"No, I think this is something he needs to do for himself. I also think that he's had a lot of people tell him that he's wrong and he's stubborn. I love that about him, but we're going to have some hard-headed disagreements in our lives, and I think he and I need to learn how to solve those without an intervention every time. As for you two, I think he needs to at least feel someone is in his corner."

"But we aren't," Dottie replied.

"You only aren't because you came to me and found out what happened. Prior to that, you were, and I think, as long as he doesn't know about this visit, he can count on you supporting him simply because he's your son. I think he knows he's wrong. Deep down, that's why he hasn't been a bulldog about this. I asked him to leave that night, and he left. And since then, he's been giving me all the space I need. So I'm choosing to read that as, at least on a subconscious level, he knows he screwed up."

"You, my dear, are a very intelligent and beautiful creature," Roger said.

"OK, Roger, hold up. I think you are a wonderful man, and I look forward to you being in my life once Jason figures this out. However, you can't call me that. As a nation, the Metis and the Indigenous were often called dogs, or mutts, or reduced to animals in an effort to justify treating us as less than a people. Add to that, women are often called creatures, pets, kittens, etc., in an effort to reduce us to inarticulate objects that have no voice. I'm going to save you from yourself and tell you to ix-nay the eature-cray before you meet any of my aunties or cousins. They. Will. Eat. You. Alive."

Roger shook his head. "Got it. You are a very intelligent and lovely woman. Better?"

"Roger, I think we will do just fine."

"You really have Dottie to thank for that. I'm about as bullheaded as our son, but she's stronger than the two of us put together, and she has shown us that you should not underestimate the power of women."

Dottie shook her head proudly. "He's come a long way, but both Roger and I will do better. Anyway, it's time for us to go. We have the boys both coming for supper tonight, and I suspect that Devin and his wife are going to tell us what they are expecting. We finally get to be grandparents!"

"Now, Dottie," Roger began, "Promise me you won't be disappointed if it's not that, but that they are moving to Venezuela instead." Roger looked at Nika, "Whenever Devin is frustrated with his mom, he threatens to up and move somewhere far away. It's a little inside joke."

"Perhaps it is for you and the boys, but I don't find it so amusing," Dottie replied stiffly. She softened and stood up to hug Nika. "Anyways, we will get out of your hair and let you get back to enjoying your weekend. I do hope to see you soon."

"Me too, Dottie."

Nika spent the rest of the day prepping and getting ready for the week coming up. She walked Bear a few times and just generally relaxed, watching Netflix and chilling with Bear. He was almost ready for her to leave him at home all day; he had just one more week of coming to work, and he should be ready. She was going to miss having him in her office.

Sunday, she spent the day catching up on cleaning and laundry. She also had a lovely long talk with her aunties but had the impression that they were holding something back from her. She resolved to call her Mom later that week and figure out what was going on.

Chapter 26

Monday morning came entirely too early, Nika thought as she packed her lunch, got all of Bear's things together, and made the trek to work. As she walked into her office, she could hear everyone over at Jessie's office talking about the karaoke that she and Cal had done after Nika had left. Curious, Nika dumped her stuff in her office, set Bear up in his dog bed, and made her way over to Jessie's office. "Hey, what happened after I left?"

"Oh, Hey, girl, how was your weekend?"

"It was good. Gabe was in for a visit, likely at Auntie's request to keep an eye on me, and then Jason's parents stopped by. Overall, I would give the weekend an 8/10."

"Wait, hold up, Jason's what stopped by?"

"His parents. So what was this about you and Cal and karaoke?"

"No no no no no no no. I want, no, I NEED to hear more about this whole Jason's parents stopped by before I share our misadventures in karaoke."

"I am pretty sure it's your turn to go first."

"Uh. No. And you are wasting time here." Jessie grinned, knowing she had Nika over the barrel on this one.

"OK FINE. So Gabe and I went out for a jog on Saturday, and when we came back, he went upstairs to shower before taking off to visit his friends in town. I was relaxing in the living room, beading a new project."

"Wait, you are beading again? Can I request something?"

"Do you want this story or not?"

"Sorry! Please go on."

"Yes, I'm beading again, and let me think about it. It may be better suited for Auntie Teresa anyway. The doorbell goes, and I check it. It's this man and woman on my front porch. I thought they were missionaries; you know how the Jehovah's Witnesses have been campaigning door to door pretty religiously lately."

Both Jessie and Nika grinned at the pun.

"So I open the door, and it's not. It's Jason's mom and dad, and they wanted to chat. Apparently, Jason gave them my address when we were going to have them over for dinner, and so they decided to stop by to see why things hadn't worked out."

"Oh my god, that is ballsy. Does Jason know?"

"Absolutely not, and Dottie and I would like to keep it that way."

"Dottie, huh?"

"Yup, we're on a first-name basis now, and you know what? I like them. I think I understand Jason's reasoning for the fight, but he's still wrong, and they agree with me on that. How did Dottie put it, "We aren't dumb," Both she and Jason's dad acknowledged that they could be a little pushy, called it stubborn, and that they have a lot to learn with regard to my culture and being politically correct, but that they were both up to the challenge and were offended that Jason thought they needed kid gloves. I honestly think it's going to take everything Dottie has not to bash his head in with a stove pot, but she promised not to clue him in, saying that she knows what the fight is about. He has to come to this on his own terms."

Jessie looked down.

"Uh oh," Nika looked at Jessie, "What is this about?"

"Let's just say Cal knows Jason is trying, and I'm worried that he won't make it right before you lose faith. I'm just asking you to hold on a little longer, is all."

Nika softened. "Oh, Jessie, I love the man. I'm beyond devastated that we are here at all. I can give him a little bit longer to figure things out."

"Good because I honestly think his heart is in the right place, and he will."

"Now about this karaoke?"

"Uh yeah, so you left, and we had a few beers and were feeling pretty feisty. So I put in a request for Sonny and Cher's I Got You Babe, and well, I got up there and started singing, and he joined in once he figured out what I was doing! It was hilarious and phenomenal. I swear to god, we were amazing and so in tune!"

Nika started laughing because Jessie was never in tune. "Will everyone agree with you about that?"

"Yes!" Jessie stated emphatically.

"Uhmmm, not a chance," came Terrell from the doorway. "I came to see how you were doing this week. Nika and I found a very content Bear, but no, Nika, I knew you were here."

"Hey, Terrell, so they both couldn't hold a tune? Or just Jessie?"

"Oh, Cal's got a great singing voice, but even he couldn't save Jessie from herself." Terrell grinned. "Cal didn't seem to mind her voice at all."

Terrell and Jessie grinned at each other, and then he turned to address Nika.

"You OK still?"

"Yeah, I'm fine."

"You had a good weekend?"

Nika hated this, and the small talk changed, as did the careful voices and reluctant questions. "Yeah!" She said with forceful enthusiasm. "My cousin Gabe came down for a visit, likely so that I wouldn't be alone, and we had a great time. Then, as I told Jessie, Jason's parents stopped by for a visit." Terrell's eyebrows shot up.

"But you haven't met them before."

"Uhh, nope. This was unexpected and new. That's for sure."

"How did that go?"

"Really well, they are good people. Then I spent the rest of the weekend just relaxing."

"OK, well, my offer from last week still stands," he replied. "If you need to take some time off and just recharge or get out of town, we'll accommodate that."

"Thanks, Terrell. I'll keep that in mind, but I'm pretty determined that work will help distract me from the crazy that my life has become."

"OK, as long as you know. I need to get back to work, and you two," he said mock seriously. "We have some due reporting this week, so let's get it finished this week. OK?"

"I was just about to leave. I need to get the Deveraux file finished, as I promised them this morning. I'll see you at lunch, Jessie."

"Yes, Ma'am!"

Nika went to her office and closed the door to get some work done with minimal interruption, and then she and Jessie headed out to lunch at their favorite lunch spot. Nika was trying to train Bear to make it through the day with no potty breaks so that he could stay home soon while she went to work. He was almost there, needing a quick break at the 3 pm break time some days.

The week whistled by pretty quickly as she and Bear got even more settled into their routine. Her workout routines with Stacey and her girls were continuously kicking her ass, but she noticed she was getting better and stronger at them. She looked up a few times to see Jason staring at her with a face she couldn't figure out. It almost looked like longing, but if it was, then why wasn't he trying harder?

After her workout on Thursday, a few girls in the group mentioned that she was looking great. "Thank y'all! I couldn't have done it without your help and support. I've never been one to really work out or find the gym a place I look forward to being in, but I love it here. It is so judgment-free and supportive, and I don't know how I would have gotten through this rough patch with you all in my corner."

Stacy smiled and half-hugged her. "Give me a few minutes, and I'll walk you out to your car." Nika smiled and nodded. If she hadn't fallen for Jason, she could have seen herself dating Stacey. Stacey was beautiful and tall and carried herself with confidence. She was very out in the open about being a lesbian and had no qualms about letting a person know just how she felt about them. Her dusky brown skin and rich chocolate eyes just mesmerized Nika, and she wasn't sure if she had imagined Stacey checking her out a few times. It was heady to think that someone like Stacey would be attracted to her, but then it was heady to think that Jason was, too.

Once Stacey packed up all her gear, they walked out to their respective vehicles, and after wishing each other a good night, they each headed home. When she walked in the door, Bear bounded over to her with a chew toy in his mouth. He clearly wanted to play, so she dropped her gear at the door and wrestled with him for the rest of the evening.

The next morning was more of the same routine. As she rushed into work with Bear, she made it known around the office that this was his last day there, that next week they would be trying him being at home all day. There were groans and awws, but she reminded people to stop by and get their cuddles in before she left for the day. Nika spent the day with her office door open as the carousel of people stopped by, making it clear that Bear was well-loved within the office, even more than she was. It would have hurt her feelings, except she understood the appeal, she couldn't resist that face either.

At three p.m., she gathered Bear's lead and made her way downstairs for Bear's last walk downtown. She walked him over to the park across the street and let him sniff and snort while they trotted along. She was busy looking at a report on her phone when suddenly she saw a shadow cross in front of her and felt Bear's leash pull tight.

She looked up and saw Bear growling at a man in a ball cap standing in her way. "I'm sorry, he's a puppy and is still learning. Do I know you?" He looked familiar, but she couldn't place him.

"Yes, Nika, you know me, and you will be coming with me right now. Drop the leash, and let's go."

"I'm sorry, but I'm not going to do that. I can't place you. Where do I know you from?"

She shoved her phone in her pocket and pulled on Bear's leash to bring him closer to her.

"It won't do you any good to cause a scene. I need you to understand that I have a gun, and I'll shoot your dog. I almost shot him that night in your house, but because the door was locked, I couldn't be sure if I would shoot you or the damn dog."

"That was you?" Nika got scared. She needed to get away right now!

"That was me. I've been trying to get your attention for a while now. You wouldn't believe the things I did to try catch your attention, I emailed your company asking for you to do my personal taxes. I delivered your pizzas and flowers, and I watched you every night. But all you were interested in was your stupid dog and that fucking guy you had staying at your place for a while. You stupid whore. Do you remember who I am now?"

"That was all you! You're crazy!" Nika realised she needed to get away from this man immediately, she looked around frantically for help but the park was empty. Why of all the times did the park have to be empty now!? "I don't remember you, and clearly you were mistaken to think you made an impression on me." His face darkened with anger.

"We met at the speed dating event," he said angrily, "I know you're just pretending you don't know who I am. I know you were as strongly affected by me as I was by you. I just know it."

"Oh, wait!" she exclaimed. "You were the racist, the first one I met."

"I AM NOT A RACIST." He shouted. A couple walking into the park stopped and stared as he shouted, she started to wave at them when he roughly grabbed her and yanked her in the opposite direction. "We need to get away from here," he muttered. "Start walking, or else I will shoot your dog," He said, raising his shirt to show the gun in his waistband.

Nika audibly gasped and froze, this gave him the momentum to pull her along and away from the people near the park entrance. She stumbled and pulled Bear along with her.

"You can drop the leash and leave the damn dog here."

"I'm not going to do that, will you really shoot my dog?" Nika protested weakly.

"Look, you bitch, you better believe I'm going to shoot your dog. If you bring it with you, I will shoot it. If it jumps up on me, I will shoot it. So you may want to quickly think about leaving that damn mutt here or else I won't be responsible when it gets hurt." He shook her violently.

"He will follow me."

Nika cried out.

"Then I will shoot it."

"How can I stop it from following me?"

"Look, tie it up to that bench."

"I can't do that!"

"Tie the fucking dog up to the bench, or so help me god, I will shoot it right now, you goddamn slut."

Nika started crying. She looked around and realized they were completely alone again, that couple must have left the park, so much for a nice sunny day at the park, no one was here enjoying the beautiful weather. She was truly alone with a madman. She bent over to tie Bear's lead onto the leg of the bench and fumbled for her phone. David was busy checking out the park, so she peeked at her phone and saw the white bubble of a text. Hoping it was Jessie, she opened it and pressed the phone in the top corner to call her friend. She only prayed he wouldn't notice.

Meanwhile, Jason decided it was time to reach out to Nika. He had been working on some things, hoping they would show her just how sorry he was and how serious he was about their future together. He sat in his truck on his break and stared at his phone before finally opening up the text box to send her the message, he knew what he had to do, he just wasn't confident in how to start.

"Hey, Nika, Jason here. I hope you didn't block me, but can we talk?"

Not even a minute later, the phone rings. He looks at the face and sees Nika's number. He frowned. Why would she call him?

He answered.

"Hey Nika, babe, I was wondering if we could…" He was interrupted by her voice. It sounded tinny, like she was far away and on speakerphone. What was going on?

"Look, can we talk about this? I tied up my dog and left him behind, as you said. I did everything you wanted me to. I don't want to go wherever you are taking me. You don't have to threaten me with that gun. What do you want? Maybe we can talk this out."

Jason's heart stopped. "Oh, baby, I need to know where you are. Come on, honey, just a few more details."

He jumped out of his truck and ran into the shop, and into the office. He snapped at the receptionist, "I need a phone, pen, and paper. NOW."

"Hey, Jason", Cal popped his head in, "what's the rush, dude?"

Jason shook his head, "I've got to listen to this. Nika's in trouble, and she's trying to tell me where he's taking her."

The receptionist's eyes went wild, and she threw a pad of paper and a pen in front of Jason and gave him the shop phone. Cal swore. "OK, dude, I'll call Jessie and figure out if Nika was at work today."

Cal ran to grab his phone. About 5 minutes later, he popped his head in the door and said, "Jessie said that Nika was there but went to take the dog out for a walk in the park. She's running out to see if she can find her."

"Tell her that Nika was forced to tie the dog to a bench. Get Bear back to her office, call 911, and have them alert the authorities of where Bear was found. It's a starting point. Right now, this chucklehead is forcing her to walk somewhere. It's muffled, but I think she's trying to give me the street address. Oh, guys, gotta gun, tell everyone that."

The receptionist gasped, Cals face darkened as he swore, talking low and fast to Jess on his phone.

Jason pleaded with the phone. "C'mon, Nika, I'm listening. Just let me know where you are."

Terrified Nika prayed that someone was listening on the other end of her phone, she hoped that she gotten through to someone who could help her and not some telemarketer. "Look, I don't even know why you are doing this. You hated me when we met. It was a complete disaster of a date. I don't understand why you are even interested in me, you called me a bitch that evening!"

"That wasn't my fault, you stupid slut. I did everything right. It was you. You talked about your heritage and culture like it's important. You decided that you didn't have to be nice to me. Well, let me tell you something, sister, you always have to be nice to me. I'm a man, and I'm more important than you. It's your job in life to keep people like me happy. Do you not understand?" He ranted furiously, Nika realised there was no talking him down, she was in serious trouble.

"How did you know where I lived?" She couldn't help but ask. She knew the speed dating organizers would have never told him that information.

"Oh, that's easy, your little blonde friend told one of the speed daters she was chatting with, where you both worked. I had the good fortune of overhearing that conversation. So I just camped out at your work until I noticed you leaving for home. I followed you, and Boom. I had everything I needed to get your attention; I knew where you worked, and I knew where you lived. I tried to be nice and send a message to you through the speed dating company, but they never responded. You don't just get to ignore nice guys like me!"

Nika snapped, "OK, OK, Mr. Nice Guy! But at least get my fucking name right, you. You called me on a cell phone! How many blocks away is your car? I can't walk all day in these heels!" She pulled back on his grip on her arm and slowed herself down, stumbling a little bit. Anything to stall for time.

He slapped her across the face. "Don't you ever take that tone with me?" He grabbed her arm and started dragging her towards his car.

"Stop hurting me! I don't want to go with you. Where are you taking me?" Nika protested forcefully, hoping that somewhere someone could hear her distress and help. "It's just a couple of blocks, and then we'll be in the car. I'm taking you somewhere nice and quiet where I can teach you how to properly treat guys like me!"

"I don't want to go with you! How many times can I say that!" She fitfully tried to twist herself out of his steel grip.

"I. Don't. Care." He wrangled her up against the car door, pushing against her with all of his body to keep her still. She shrunk away from him, the feeling of him pressing on her filling her with fear and disgust.

Using his car fob, he unlocked the door of his car. Nika changed her track and stopped, and said, "Is that a Beemer?" Perhaps if she distracted him she could buy some time.

Proudly, he said. "Got your attention, huh? You like them loaded, don't you, you little bitch. All you women care about the money."

"It's a beautiful car that's a great shade of blue. Is that a 5 series? Can't be a lot of them on the road." Hopefully, someone was on the other end of her phone and listening, she would try to give them as many clues as she could. She didn't care what he thought of her, she would do whatever it took to stall.

"There aren't, not around here. Now get in the car bitch."

"I still don't want to go anywhere with you."

"I said I don't care," as he started attempting to push her head down and into the car.

Jason looked up at Cal and the receptionist. "He's some guy she met at the speed dating event I met her at. He sent her a private message through them. Maybe tell Jessie that, and she will remember? He said he overheard Jessie talking about where she worked, and he just camped out there until he managed to tail Nika home one night. Maybe tell Jessie it's not her fault."

The receptionist piped up, "I'm on the phone with 911. Cal and I figured it would be faster if I called than if Cal relayed everything to Jessie. Do you have anything I need to tell them?"

"Yeah, he's in a Series 5 BMW in blue, he's downtown near her work, and he's currently trying to stuff her in the car. They walked about 2-3 blocks from the park, as near as I could figure. He said a couple of blocks. He wants to take her somewhere quiet. Oh, and he called her a cell phone?"

Cal repeated that to Jessie. "Whoa, whoa, whoa! Calm down? What?"

Cal looked at Jason. "Nika had a disaster of an opener with this guy at the speed dating thing. Really clueless, insulted her left, right, and center, and then got insulted that she was insulted. He messaged the speed dating company to send her a message, which they did, where he further insulted her, told her to see a personal trainer and lose about 20 pounds, and then he might consider dating her. Anyways, he called her Nokia in the email. Everyone thought it was a little humorous that he wanted to be taken so seriously, but couldn't even get her name right. Jessie is on the phone with the speed dating company and relaying this information. She said she may have a name soon. However, the speed dating company may need to call the police with that information because of privacy issues."

"I don't fucking care how they do it, just get someone that name and fast. You don't think that guy would be stupid enough to take her back to his place, would you?"

Cal shrugged. "I don't know man, I don't understand why anyone does any of this."

Chapter 27

Nika put up a bit of a fight when he stuffed her into the backseat of the car. He had enabled the child locks so she wouldn't be able to leave the vehicle once he shut the door. She got a few good kicks into his knees and screamed loud for anyone to hear before he managed to shut the door on her. It wasn't enough. There was no one around.

As he limped around to the driver's seat, she realized she had no way of getting out. He had prepped the car by putting a mesh wall up between the backseat and the front seat. Clearly he had been planning this for a while. She felt sick. She was stuck. She remembered reading somewhere that letting someone take you away to another location was very bad, so she started hitting and kicking the glass windows while screaming at the top of her lungs. It terrified her that there was no one around to notice her distress.

He got into the driver's seat and shouted, "SHUT THE FUCK UP ALREADY, YOU GODDAMN BITCH." As he drove off, he continued to shout at her about how no one cared and no one was going to save her. He really was crazy, she trembled, hoping that he wasn't right, and that someone would come to her rescue.

Jason murmured, "Oh, honey, I care, and I'll save you. Just hold on, give me something, anything!"

Nika hit the cage really hard behind David's ear. "Where are you taking me?" She screamed. "Why are we leaving downtown?"

"Look bitch! I told you, I just want to take you somewhere quiet where I can teach you how to treat a real man properly."

"You don't get to lay a hand on me."

"That's what you think." He snarled, "I got it all planned out, I'm going to teach you how to be real respectful to your betters. It's going to take time clearly, but I'm going to enjoy all the training I'm going to do and when I'm done, you're gonna be really happy to do whatever it takes to make me happy."

Jason slammed his fist on the counter and looked up from the phone, his eyes were dark and intense, "He's leaving downtown. We need to figure out where they are going and fast before we lose them. This asshole is going to pay."

The receptionist looks up at him and Cal, "The police have identified him and are on their way to his home. Hopefully, they can figure out what he has planned once they get a look around." The receptionist shivered. "This guy sounds dangerous."

"I want to know who he is!" Jason growled. "I can't just sit here and wait." The receptionist shrugged, they won't tell me, all they said was that they have identified the perpetrator and figured out his place of residence and are headed there. Jason growled and ran out of the shop, jumping into his truck. Cal right on his heels, protesting. "Look, dude, I know you want to go racin' off somewhere, but we just don't know where to go."

"Cal, I gotta do something." Jason put the phone back to his ear. He could hear Nika arguing about getting out of the car. Clearly, they had arrived at wherever this man wanted to take her.

Nika kicked and argued with David as he tried to pull her out of the car. In the shuffle, her phone fell out of her pocket. David picked it up and looked at her with a vicious expression. "You BITCH!" he slapped her across the face. He then put the phone up to his ear and said, "I don't know who you are, but say goodbye to Nika. She's mine now."

Jason growled as the phone disconnected. He looked at Cal with devastated eyes. "He found the phone."

David threw the phone on the ground and ground it under his heel. Nika could see the glass shattering and the case turning into twisted, useless metal. There went her chances.

Cal worked on calming Jason down.

"Hey buddy, I know. I mean, if it were Jessie, I would just be tearing my hair out right now. I get it. Jessie is devastated, and I'm trying to reassure her and help you, but it's a lot. So bear with me."

"BEAR! Cal, I gotta go and get Bear. He's the first thing Nika is going to want to see when this is all over." Jason swung his truck door open and jumped into the cab. "Are you coming or not? You can console Jessie while I get Bear. I can't just stand here and do nothing Cal, I gotta go."

"Are you sure that you're the first thing she's going to want to see?" Cal shook his head, "Maybe slow down a little bit here. I can check with Jessie and see what she thinks."

"Dude, man, none of that matters. I love her, you know? I'll say I'm sorry until the end of time if that will bring her home safe and sound."

"But what are you saying I'm sorry for?" Cal asked seriously. "Because you haven't been saying too much about what you've done wrong, and dude you know I think you messed up."

Jason sighed, "Cal, I know what I did. I've known for a while. I've been working on an apology that I was planning to show her this weekend. I just thought I had more time. Oh crap! Her family! Cal, I gotta make some calls." Jason frantically reached for his phone.

"How do you know her family? I mean, I know you met them once, but I didn't realize you had their contact information."

"Nah, dude, I've been working with them on the apology bit. Just let me call her Kokum really quickly."

"You've been what? Her Kokum what? What's going on man?" Calvin pressed curiously.

"Cal, I knew I fucked up, like the minute the words were out of my mouth I knew I fucked up. I just couldn't seem to extricate myself out of the argument. As Nika always told me, it was my job to educate myself, so I reached out to her cousin Gabe, he gave me his number in case I had any questions about taking care of Bear. Gabe connected me with Nika's Kokum and Aunties and I've been working with them ever since. "

Cal dropped silent. He couldn't figure out half of what Jason meant, but he sure hoped that Jason was on the right track. He never saw a couple more fated for each other. He also called Jessie to let her know that they would be stopping by her work to get Bear and Jessie.

He overheard Jason on the phone. "Hey, Mrs. Patience. I gotta, no, let me get this out, that guy has got Nika. The police are chasing down some leads. He nabbed her at the park right outside of her work as she was taking Bear for a quick walk. Yeah, I know. Yeah. You'll call everyone, right? I gotta go. I'll get her back, I promise. No, I know, I know. I will do my best. Yes, I will. OK, Gabe still has the key? Then yeah, go to the house. We will bring her home."

Jason hung up, "Her family is heading to the house. I'm going to go and get Bear, and then I'm...WAIT. She had her smartphone with her, and it was on. Can you have Jessie call 911 to relay that information to the police, then can you call the last number I dialed on my phone?" as he tosses his phone into Cal's lap "and tell Patience that little bit of information, ask her if anyone in the family could use find my iPhone to locate Nika. The guy is parked somewhere now. I'm going to head into the city and pick up Bear."

"And Jessie, I told her we would pick her up too."

Jason nodded.

"OK, Nika, babe, we're on our way, and we will get to you."

Nika was frozen in fear as David dragged her into the house. She knew once she was inside, her chances were getting slimmer and slimmer of someone saving her. She had watched all the true crime documentaries; she knew the first mistake was letting them get you alone in a place no one knew about.

She started screaming again, and David grabbed her by the hair and slapped her forcefully across the cheek. She stopped screaming in shock, and he nodded happily. Her ears were ringing so forecfully, she couldn't hear a thing he said.

"That's going to leave a bruise. The first of many, I suspect, you seem to be a bit of a dumb slut. I'm going to likely end up giving you more bruises as I teach you what's good for you."

Nika stared at him dully, still shocked that she was in this situation. She couldn't believe that this man was so angry at her , and willing, no, excited even to hurt her. She didn't know what she had done to deserve this. What had she ever done to him, she asked herself. She wouldn't have to wonder long as he erupted into a tirade of every perceived slight and insult she had given him the past few months. As the list grew longer and more improbable, she realized that he was truly unwell and that posed a significant danger to her. She had to get out of here and fast! While she was hopeful that whoever she had dialed was frantically trying to find her, she couldn't depend on it, now that her phone was destroyed, her one link to safety was gone. She could feel the despair leaking into her body as she tearfully contemplated her options. She was just going to have to figure out a way to escape. She couldn't let this man get the better of her.

David grabbed her by the hair and yanked her up, shocking her out of her reverie. She grabbed his hands, trying to free herself as he dragged her to a windowless room. He threw her in, and her hip slammed against the bed frame as she fell to the floor and hit her head on the bedside table. She gasped in pain as she brought her hands up to cradle her head gently, her hip throbbing from the impact.

"Think about what you have done and how awful you have been to me. Think about how you can make it up to me," With a long lingering look on her lips, David sneered "I have a few ideas of what you can do to show your penitence for these insults. You will come to love pleasing me." She shivered with disgust and fear as he closed the door and locked it from the outside.

Nika allowed herself some time to cry while she pummeled at the locked door. Soon her fists began to throb in tandem with her hip. She sat down gingerly on the bed while she considered her options. Her brain almost felt too fuzzy to think clearly. Was she concussed? Did she need medical help?

Time seemed to travel so slowly while she was trapped; her head was bleeding slightly, and she mopped it up with a corner of the bed sheet while contemplating her surroundings and possible escape. How far was she willing to go to get out of here? Could she hurt him? Could she kill him? In her solitude, her bravado told her that she could do both those things. Suddenly, she could feel what felt like loud noises and bangs on the other side of the door. She didn't know what was happening, but it sounded chaotic enough, she was hopeful it meant someone was here to help her. She ran to the door, screaming and shouting, banging her fists frantically to gain anyone's attention. "I'm here! I'm here! He has me trapped in this room. Please come get me!"

Something big hit the other side of the door, and she fell to the floor and ducked, screaming, "HE HAS A GUN!"

Crying in desperation and curled up in a ball, trying to make herself as small as possible, she hoped that whatever was happening, someone would come and let her out soon.

Suddenly, the door opened to two police officers crowding the door and looking in. She sat up and started sobbing hysterically, dropping her head into her hands. She repeated "Thank you" over and over while one of them draped a blanket around her shoulders.

Meanwhile, Jason and Cal raced to pick up Bear and Jessie. Once downtown, Jessie hopped into their truck with Bear, settling him in beside her as Jason and Cal argued about what to do next. Did they head back to Nika's house and wait with the rest of Nika's family? Did they drive around and do a little canvassing, sleuthing of their own? Jessie kept trying to interrupt the arguing men, to no avail. Finally, in frustration, she whistled high and long until they both shut up and stared at her.

"Did you know that Terrell used to drag race in his day?"

Cal and Jason looked at her, stupefied.

"Did you know that one of the few habits that he still has from those days is to carry a police scanner? "

"Aren't those illegal?"

"Yes, but he has one, and he's given it to me. You know, desperate times, desperate measures."

Cal leaned back, grabbed her by the neck, and brought her in for a deep kiss. "You know I love you, right?"

"I believe you've told me that before."

"What?! You two have shared the L word? Not even Nika and I got that far! We were starting to talk about how much we cared." Jason shared sadly.

Jessie glanced coolly at Jason. "We know."

"Uh oh. I was planning on it. Had this big surprise about how I was going to apologize and everything. Scouts honor."

Jessie sighed. "As happy as that makes me feel", she rummaged in her bag for the police scanner and handed it to Cal to set up. "You realize all Nika needed was an I'm sorry, and things would have been fine. Like you've wasted so much time, dude."

Jason had the grace to look hang-dogged. "Yeah, I know."

Cal shushed them. "Hey, listen to this."

"10-64 At the residence of 417 Lombardy, one person injured, possibly two, kidnapping in progress, suspect apprehended."

"Betcha, that's them!" Jason shouted.

Jessie piped up, "You're going to want to turn left at the next intersection. I got the address on my maps, and we'll get there in about 30 minutes if traffic doesn't work against us."

Cal looked at Jason with a grin, "Looks like you got your girl."

Jason grinned back. "Well, I still have to get her. You know, she might be a little mad at me."

Jessie interrupted. "God, you two are the worst. Could you get me to my best friend pronto, please?!"

"On it." Jason retorted.

"I'm going to be really upset if this isn't Nika." Jessie moaned.

"You can't think like that, honey." Cal squeezed her hand.

It was a very tense drive to the address.

Nika let the police officers lead her to the back of an ambulance, averting her eyes to the body on the floor as they moved her past David.

"Is he.... dead?"

"Nope. He's just incapacitated. We got him in the shoulder, and we're just keeping him immobile until we are ready to take him away. Don't worry about him, young lady. He's going to be going away for a long time, it's one thing to kidnap a person, it's a whole other thing to shoot at a police officer. By the way, I've got two officers who want to talk to you. They said they were helping you with a stalking incident and that he may be the guy."

"Oh yeah, he's the guy." she scowled.

"Great, you're going to have to answer some of their questions and help them do a report. I'm going to leave you with them and get back in there to process the scene. You did great," he said with a pat on her upper arm.

As the two officers started peppering her with questions, the other police officers led David out of the house and into the waiting police car. She paused in answering questions and watched the procession of police officers as they escorted David in cuffs to the waiting vehicle. She began shivering and trembling. The one police officer beside her was touching her arm and directing her attention back to him. "Why don't you not watch that? Pay attention to us and forget about him. You are safe now."

"I feel like if I take my eyes off him, something will happen."

"Nothing is going to happen. He's going to get into the vehicle and be taken in for processing. Then we are going to collect the evidence, including your report, so that we can put him away for a very long time."

"People like him don't seem to go away for a very long time."

The police officer nodded, "Well, he shot at us, so that helps."

She nodded her head back. "Yeah, that helps."

"I'm not saying that it's right, but it is what it is. I do need you to answer these questions so that we can do what we need to ensure he has a long holiday courtesy of the judicial system."

Suddenly, the police officers jerked their necks to look behind them. As Nika glanced past them, she saw Jessie, Bear, Cal, and Jason running towards her. Bear reached her first and just about bowled her over as Jessie grabbed her in for a deep hug. "Oh my god, girl, I was so fucking worried. I've never been so scared in my life."

"Miss? Could you maybe control your dog? We need to finish processing the crime scene and that includes talking to your friend here." The police officers interrupted. "Could you please step aside and give us about 10 or 20 more minutes. Then we will let you get to your little reunion."

Nika handed Bear back to Jessie as she answered the last of their questions. Jessie, Jason, and Cal stood off to the side, listening in on the conversation. She could see Cal and Jason getting angrier and angrier as they overheard what had happened to her.

The one police officer interrupted her narrative. "Has anyone looked at your head since you bumped it?"

"No, they brought me to you. I may have forgotten to tell them I bumped it when they were doing a checkup. I was just so scared."

"OK, lets get that looked at right now, I think you're going to have a nasty bruise from the swelling I'm already seeing. Are there any other injuries?"

"Well I hit my hip when he threw me in the room, and I was banging on the doors for a while, I quit because my fists started to hurt." Nika mentioned.

"Let's get those looked at as well. We'll do that now if you don't mind," motioning for a paramedic still on scene. "Can you look at her head? She bumped it on the bedside table and said it was bleeding. Maybe also check her hands and hip. " the officer instructed.

He motioned at another police officer. "She knocked her head on the bedside table. Could you make sure forensics catches it?"

"Oh, I also wiped my bleeding head on the sheets on the bed."

"Check that, too."

"She's got a nasty bump but doesn't seem to be concussed and won't need stitches. Her hip will likely bruise a nasty little bruise and her hands are a little beat up. Nothing some rest and care won't fix up. I still recommend her going into the hospital for a quick checkup, though." the EMT reports.

"Thanks" Nika quietly stated as the paramedic continued to poke at her head. She winced in pain at a particularly sensitive spot.

The police officer looks at her. "Any chance you will go to the hospital?"

"I feel fine. If you insist, I will go, but I'd rather not. I just want to go home with my friends."

Jason piped up. "I can take her, Officer, but her family is waiting for her at her house. I believe her mom is a nurse."

"My what?"

Jessie burst. She couldn't take it anymore. "Oh my god, Nika, we were so scared. You called Jason, and he could hear everything. He heard you mention where you left Bear, and I picked him up. They came and got me, and we." The police officer interrupted Jessie.

"Yeah, how did you get here?"

Cal shrugged. "Police scanner, a friend of a friend gave it to us."

"I'm going to have to confiscate that, you realize?"

Cal shrugged again. "It's done its job."

"Anyways", Jessie began, clearly irritated with being interrupted. We listened to the police scanner and figured out it was you."

Jason piped up. "I called your family and told them what was happening; things were moving too fast for the authorities to let them know. I told them I would bring you home. If that's ok with you. Your mom, aunties, and Kokum are waiting at home for you."

"How did they get into my house?" Nika asked.

"Gabe still has the key from that weekend he spent at your place, he's going to meet them there and let them in." Jason added.

Nika nodded thoughtfully. "I guess thank you for doing that. I do appreciate that."

The police officer was getting more irritated by the minute. "Look, I think we're done here. You," he said, pointing at Cal, "are going to take me to the truck for that police scanner, and I'm going to go and write up my report. I want you", pointing at Nika, "to get medical care, whether it's your mom or the hospital, do not go to sleep without having that closely looked at and dealt with." Nika nodded her assent while her friends promised to look after her.

"You are a very lucky young lady. You have some really good friends here. Now I'm going to leave, and you two are going to kiss and make up." He glanced at Jason, "I knew you two weren't done when I saw her last after the break-in." Nika looked down at the ground and smiled softly.

Cal piped up, looking at Jason "Hey do Jessie and I a favor and drop us off at the shop on your way to Nika's. I'll get my truck, and we will meet you both at Nika's house. That will give you two a chance at some privacy before you walk into that circus. We all know it's going to be a circus once you two get there."

Jason's phone rang, and when he looked at it, it was his parents.

"I gotta take this."

"Hey, Ma. Look, now is not a good time. No, I'm fine. Nika got into a spot of trouble, and I'm with her right now. Ma, I'll fill you in later. What? No! No," deep sighs. "Ma, she was kidnapped today. The police just found her and apprehended the guy. NO! I didn't hit him! Yes, it would have felt damn good, though."

Cal exploded in laughter, and even the police officer smirked. He looked at Nika. "You have your hands full, you know."

She shook her head in assent. "Oh, I know; I've known for a while now."

The police officer finally walked to his car, where his partner was waiting. Nika shivered in the cooling air as night was quickly approaching. She waited patiently for Jason to finish talking to his parents. When he hung up, he was shaking his head as he walked towards her. He grabbed the blanket and pulled her in close to him. "Don't ever scare me like that again." He whispered furiously as he hugged her so tight she could feel every tense muscle. As he pulled away, he cupped her face. "We have a lot to talk about."

She nodded. "Yes, we do."

He looked up at Cal, "Hey man, let's get on the road and get you two dropped off at your truck so that I can finally have a moment alone with my girl here."

Nika craned her neck around. "Your girl?"

Jason winked and hugged her close. "I'm that confident that we will figure this out."

"OK then." She wondered if he knew that she had already met his parents, probably not, based on his end of the call.

The drive back to the shop was filled with laughter and this low, thrumming tension. Nika knew that she and Jason were going to have a very serious discussion, and that worked on her nerves the entire drive. Both Jessie and Cal knew, too, and their antics to try and de-escalate the growing tension only managed to make Nika hyper-aware of the situation. Once back at the shop, Cal hopped out of the truck with palpable relief and grabbed Jessie by the waist to pull her into his arms. He slammed the doors, shouting, "Thanks for the ride! See you at the house!"

They could hear Jessie screaming, "I wasn't done talking!" and Cal shouting back, "Yes, you were! We will see them at the house right away anyway!"

Nika laughed as Jason turned in the driver's seat to look back at her. "Do you want to come up here in the front? Or are you determined to stay back there with Bear while I chauffeur you?"

Her face softened into a shy smile. "Uhmm, how about both Bear and I come to the front?" He leaned over to open the door while she got out of the back of the truck carrying Bear in her arms. She hopped in the front, closed the door, and turned to look at him.

His face got serious. "OK, Nika, I uh…" he sighed heavily. "Look, I'm stubborn." she laughed. "No, look, I'm stubborn, and I probably should have apologized a while ago, but I wanted so damn bad to be right, even though I knew the minute the words left my mouth that I had made a huge mistake. Like HUGE."

She opened her mouth to interrupt, and he put his finger on her mouth to stop her.

"I'm so sorry." She opened her mouth again. "No, please, Nika, let me get this out. I need to say these things, and I don't want to forget any of them. I had this whole thing planned, and now I have to wing it, and I'm unprepared, so let me just talk."

She closed her mouth and waited.

"I'm sorry. I'm sorry I made you feel unworthy of me or my parents. I'm sorry that I made you feel like I felt you were less than me. I'm sorry that I asked you to do that. I'm sorry that I defended my actions and then got angry when you didn't accept my bullshit reasoning. I have these mad strong feelings for you, and I felt stuck between them and my need to protect my parents, as well as" he grimaced, "protect people FROM my parents. Man, they are well-intentioned but a freaking PR nightmare."

Nika grinned and waited.

"I just want to kiss your lips, hug you, and have you back in my arms. I want to live with you and be with you. I want us back, the laughs, the gym, the smiles, the sex, god damn, I miss the sex. I want you, babe, and Bear, back where you belong, with me."

"OK," Nika said.

"That's it?"

"Well, can I talk now?"

Jason growled, grabbed her neck and pulled her close, rubbing her cheek with his cheek. "Yeah, you can talk now."

"I accept your apology, and I know from talking to Cal and from conversations you and I have had about your parents that you are a good son who is deeply devoted to them. While I acknowledge that it must have felt a little bit like being trapped between two good intentions, I will say you chose the wrong dog in the fight, and I accept your apology for that."

He nodded ruefully.

"I will love and respect your parents, and I will love and respect your devotion to them and your need to be a good son."

"I wasn't always, you know."

"I bet. But I'm pretty sure that if they were pressed on it, they would admit that your girl comes first. They put each other first at some point, and if you want to be with me, I have to come first. I will always work with you to make it as easy as possible, but I have to come first; otherwise, we don't have a relationship."

"I got you, babe."

"If you had just said, 'Wear whatever you want, be you,' however, I am worried about how my parents will react, and I'm worried they will say the wrong thing or hurt you.' I can work with that. I won't change anything, but I'll be empathetic to your worries, and I will work to help you communicate with them about where they went wrong. Everyone's allowed to make mistakes and learn."

He sighed. "I know, babe, I know. I just freaked out, and then you got defensive, and I freaked out more."

"You understand why I got defensive, right?"

"Yeah, babe, I have had a lot of time to do my own learning and thinking lately, and I understand that you had every right to be upset, and I had less of a right to be upset. I just didn't articulate myself well, and I apologize for that, too."

"Wow," Nika said. "Articulate, huh?"

"I've been reading."

"Yeah?"

"I've been talking and learning."

"I can see that. I'm proud of you."

"Oh, babe, you just wait and see. You haven't seen anything yet," he grinned. "Come here." He looped his arm around her waist and pulled her into his lap, making sure the steering wheel didn't dig into her sore hip. He dropped his mouth down and went in for a deep soul searching kiss. "Oh babe, how I have missed that. Are we good?"

"We are good", she affirmed. He frowned and pushed her back. "What?" she demanded.

"Honey, you got small. Where's all that junk?"

She scoffed. "I did not get small. It's right there in your hands, you perv."

"Oh, you've lost a size at least. I swear. I'm not sure if I'm OK with this."

She swatted at him. "Look, I work out, I have a deep connection with the gym, and I..." she broke into giggles.

He grinned at her. "You are beautiful to me, no matter what. Doesn't matter. But I will say that I was really proud that you stood your ground and kept coming to the gym even through our issues. That turned me on a lot and helped me to realize really quickly what a fucking fool I was being."

"Well, I think the lack of appetite because I was missing you definitely helped, too."

"I can't have you wasting away. I sure hope they ordered pizza."

"Jason. I love you."

"Yeah, babe. I know." He turned away and started the truck. She wrinkled her nose in confusion. She honestly thought he was going to say it back to her. Maybe she was more concussed than she thought and was misreading all the signals she thought she saw.

The drive back to her house was short and sweet. She cuddled Bear while Jason held one of her hands, and she went through the whole conversation in her head to figure out where she went wrong.

As they pulled up into her driveway, she was shocked at the plethora of vehicles parked in front of her house. Did everyone come to visit?

Jason got out of the truck and came over to her side, where he opened the door, pulled her out of the truck into his arms, and gave her a big kiss. He looked into her eyes and said, "Last moment alone for a while, I imagine. Everyone is going to want to visit and go over the events all night tonight. I'm just telling you now upfront that I'll be spending the night with you tonight."

"You don't have to. They caught the guy."

"Oh, believe me, I do have to. It has nothing to do with them catching the guy." He pulled her close for a quick, hard kiss.

OK, she thought, that's how it is.

She walked Bear up the steps with Jason behind her, and she walked into her home. Her mom and Aunties raced up to her and pulled her into a huge hug.

"Oh my god, sweetie, we were so worried!"

"What happened? Are you OK? Did he hurt you?"

"I'm fine, Mom, Auntie Teresa, and Auntie Grace. I'll be OK, but I think it's going to take time. I'm glad that I have Bear and Jason here with me." She glanced up at him shyly while she ran through what happened quickly.

Her mom pulled her onto the living room couch. "Someone give me some light; I need to check her head."

"Mom! Give me a second, would you?"

Gabe leaned around the corner and shone the flashlight of his smartphone over her head while her mom pawed at her.

"Mom! OW. That's the spot!" she feebly tried to smack her hand away.

Her mom's hands gentled as she parted the hair and gasped, hemmed, and hawed. "Well, I don't think you need stitches, but you've got a decent bump there, and you definitely split the skin a bit. Someone should probably stay with you in case you are concussed."

"That'll be me, Ma'am." Jason piped up.

"Oh, Maarsi Jason," Holly murmured. "Nice to see you again. How are the fingers? still cramping?" Nike frowned confusedly, she could tell her mom was overwhelmed with her slipping into Michif as she thanked Jason, but what was all this talk about fingers and cramping? What was going on?

"Nope, those stretching exercises are working fantastic, thanks!"

Holly grabbed Nika's chin and forced her to look up at her. "Are you OK with Jason staying, or should I have Gabe stay?"

Gabe sauntered over. "I'm cool, cousin. I can stay if you need me to." He leaned down for a hug.

"No, Mom, Jason and I talked it out. We're OK. He can stay."

"Are you sure?" Holly asked seriously.

"Mom! I'm sure. I'm very sure."

"OK then." She patted Nika's shoulder and leaned in for a long hug while she whispered in her ear. "I was so scared for you. Don't scare me like that again, and don't let this one slip through your fingers."

Nika pulled back. "Speaking of fingers, when did you two talk about cramping fingers? I don't remember that coming up the day you met?"

Jason looked away for a minute, and Holly muttered, "Are you sure? I'm almost positive it came up during that visit, right, Jason?"

He had the grace to look embarrassed.

Just then, Dottie and Roger came around the corner from the kitchen, and Jason had a look of utter shock and panic.

"Mom? Dad? What in the heck are you two doing here? I told you not to come. This wasn't the best time for you to meet Nika!"

Roger smiled a big smile and came up to hug Nika. "Son, if you had given your mom 5 minutes to explain, she would have told you that we have already met Nika. We stopped by here about two weeks ago." He looked askance at his wife and Nika. "We wanted to meet the girl who had the power to make you the happiest man alive and yet the most miserable bastard ever."

Jason spluttered. "How did you? What? I don't understand."

Nika looked at him softly and patted his hand. "You gave them my address because they were going to come over that night for dinner. So they had my address, and your mom convinced your dad to stop by and drop in for a quick coffee."

"They just showed up?" Jason glared at his mom.

"Yes, son," Dottie said nonplussed. "We did."

"And you let them in?"

Nika nodded. "Yes, because they were worried about you."

"You had a stalker! You should have been worried about you!"

"Jason, calm down right now," Dottie exclaimed. "It was fine. It was lovely and fine. We talked about the fight you two had and about how much she loved you." Nika blushed, remembering that Jason had yet to say the words back to her.

"We had a little talk about Metis history and sign language, and we met the adorable Gabe over there." Dottie waved at Gabe, standing next to his father, with a beer in his hand. He frowned and waved back. He looked at Nika and mouthed, "Adorable?"

Nika and Uncle Mike laughed.

Dottie responded exasperatedly, "YES, Adorable! I've been practicing my lip reading, too, by the way, young man! You'll have to figure out other ways to get by me!"

Everyone laughed.

Dottie looked at Nika. "I'm incredibly sorry about what happened to you this afternoon. I hope you are feeling better soon, and if my son gives you any more trouble, you call me. Got that?"

"Yes, Dottie", Nika laughed and stood up for a long hug.

"Welcome to the family, dear. I hope Jason manages to keep you, but if he doesn't, you're still family to me."

"Oh, thanks, Mom!" Jason muttered.

"Son, if you want to keep her, get to it!"

Everyone laughed again. Dottie was a treasure, and Nika could see the love in their eyes as they teased and ribbed each other. It was no wonder Jason worried about them; there was a real deep love there, something Nika would be honored to share.

Suddenly, she felt a hand on her shoulder. She looked down and saw that it was her Kokum. "Kokum!" Nika leaned down for a hug, letting her grandma envelop her in warmth and the smells of sage, leather, and fire. She felt completely at peace and at home as she breathed in deeply and settled into the hug.

Her Kokum pulled away and looked at Jason. "Young man, I believe you have something you wanted to say to Nika?"

Jason didn't look too pleased to be put on the spot. He took a deep breath and muttered, "OK. Here goes."

Nika watched him curiously.

He turned to her and looked at her with great concentration. He lifted up his hands and started signing. "Nika, I wanted to say again how sorry I am for the argument that we had. I never meant to hurt your feelings the way that I did."

Nika gasped and brought her hand up to her mouth. "How?" she asked.

Just then, Cal and Jessie walked into the now-crowded living room. Cal shushed Jessie and pointed at Nika and Jason, who were sitting on the couch. Jessie turned to look and gasped.

Cal shook his head as if to say he would answer that later. Nika's Kokum nodded in approval and said, "Go on, Son, you are more than ready for this."

Jason continued to sign. "When I realized that I needed to apologize to you, I also realized that I had to do something I hadn't done yet. I had to come to you and meet you where you are. I needed to make sure that I did everything in my power to be a complete support system for you. And because of that, you need to see these words from me, in sign language.." He took a deep breath, noticing that Nika had tears in her eyes. He reached up and wiped them gently from her cheeks. "Nika", he continued to sign. "I love you. I love you now, I love you tomorrow, I promise to love you for as long as you will let me."

Nika's breath caught on a sob; no one had ever done this for her before.

She nodded her head yes and launched herself into his lap, not caring who was watching. Jason caught her and held her close to his chest, curling her up in his arms and just holding her. His arms had missed her for so long that he never wanted to let go. He looked up at Cal and just grinned. "Taking notes?"

"Ah, bud, I'm wayyyyyyyy ahead of you on that."

Everyone laughed. Kokum Patience patted his hand and said, "You were wonderful. Still going to come for those lessons?"

"Absolutely, Miss Patience."

She grinned. "Judging from the way my granddaughter is acting right now, you can call me Kokum, too. It won't be long, I'm thinking."

"Oh, Kokum!" Nika sighed exasperatedly.

"He's your person, dear. He always was and always will be."

"Yes, Kokum."

"Now, Holly, Grace, and Teresa! Who's going to get these old bones home?"

"Ma, let me say good night to my daughter. She was kidnapped this afternoon, if you remember, and I'll give Jason some instructions to watch over her this evening, and then I'll take you home."

"Holly, take your time." Grace interrupted, "I'll take Mom home."

Everyone started to break up and headed for the door in a rush. People came over for hugs while others cleaned up the kitchen. Jessie and Cal promised to come over early the next day and spend some time just relaxing before they hit up the gym. Jason wasn't sure if Nika should go until her head injury was cleared up. Nika really wanted her life to get back to normal as fast as possible and was already arguing that she could handle a day in the gym.

Gabe gave his cousin a quick peck on the cheek and a strong handshake for Jason and herded his parents out the door with a flurry of goodbyes.

Holly went into the kitchen with Jason to write down some notes about what to look for and how to care for Nika. Nika hugged Bear as she said goodbye to her Kokum and Aunt Grace.

She wandered back into the kitchen with Bear toddling behind. She saw Jason and Holly chatting on the island while Dottie and Roger cleaned up, and she got a glimpse into what their future with their blended families would be like. It was a good scene, a good feeling.

She leaned against the island and smiled as she watched everyone. Jason looked up from the paper Holly was writing instructions on and winked at Nika. She grinned back.

Dottie put away the last of the dishes and went over to her son.

She gave him a strong hug and said, "You are happy again. I like seeing this. It puts my heart at ease. You take care of her, protect her, and nurture her. All your father and I have ever wanted for you was to find happiness in your life and the love that we have found in ours. We were relieved when you found your career, as you were so aimless before. We are ecstatic that you've found your person. All is right in the world, and we can relax knowing our boys are in good hands and good places." Jason hugged her back.

"Thanks, Ma."

Roger moved in and also hugged Jason. "Your mother, in the usual fashion, said it all and said it best. I have nothing to add other than I love you son, and I'm proud of you. Nika is a wonderful addition to our family."

Dottie and Roger came over to give her hugs. Dottie looked up at Jason as she put on her coat and said, "This time, honey, give up the apartment, make the leap. There's no going back."

Jason chuckled. "We'll talk about it. This is Nika's house. She has the final say."

Nika came up behind him as he walked them to the door and wrapped her arms around his waist. She poked her head around him and said, "We can talk about it."

Dottie looked pleased and excited. "That's all I ask."

As they finally shut the door on Nika's Mom, Jason stood by the door watching her get into her car and drive away to make sure she got on her way safely.

Nika went about the house, putting Bear outside and shutting off the lights.

Tears silently fell down her face, and she thought about the beautiful pledge of love Jason had made for her. No one had ever done something like that for her.

Jason grabbed her and pulled her into his arms. "Ready to go to bed? Wait, why are you crying?"

She smiled. "Happy tears. No one has ever taken the time to learn sign language for me."

"Oh, honey, you are more than worth it. I'm learning Michif, too, but it's a lot harder. I'm pretty sure I flunked French in high school."

Nika giggled. "I'll settle for a sign language right now."

She called Bear to follow them up the stairs. Jason looked at her as he carried her up the stairs.

"I'll settle for learning all that I can for the rest of our lives."

"Deal"

As he walked into the bedroom and settled her on the bed, following her down and giving her a deep soul-dragging kiss, he pulled back and looked into her eyes as he said,

"I love you, babe, and I look forward to spending the rest of my life showing you all the ways that I love you."

"I love you too, Jason."